Teeny Tiny
Dragon's Tales

Robert Scudder

1-0

This book has been published by Thomas Trimble of TomsBooks

All rights belong to the author

Visit our website at www.ttrimb1e.com

Printed in the United States of America

First Printing: Dec 2022

Kindle Direct Publishing

ISBN-13 979-83636185-8-1

Contents

Dedication

Dedicated with love to all children. Regardless the age of their bones.

Prologue

Dragon's Manifestation.

Our storyteller begins the telling of this tale, as thus...

"Now where to begin? Perhaps, to commence with the classic time-honored, traditional introduction? Oh, why not? Very well then. Let us begin...

Once upon a time...

A long time ago...

In a place, said to be very far away...

Legend has it, at least according to whispered stories about certain treasures of legend, archeologists have recently unearthed an enigmatic book of gold. A fabled manuscript once thought lost forever. Long forgotten by time. It has been said to be buried somewhere, deep under the ruined Library of Alexandria. Entombed therein rests one, and only one, unimaginably beyond priceless, hand-engraved text. Remarkably, the tome is printed on three thousand one hundred forty-four leaves of pure solid gold. Talk about your priceless treasure! Obviously, the author intended his work to last for many generations! The single, cryptic-in-nature manuscript, is rumored to be safely secured, or more than likely hidden, for practically all of perpetuity.

It was found the unbelievably priceless artifact, containing the most unlikely of legends. Somehow spinning itself, some of the most fantastic fables that were ever fabricated. One fabled legend, in particular, concerns certain mysterious miniature dragons; mighty magical, albeit memory-challenged master magicians, the strangest of pale blue visitors faring from even stranger yet, faraway places, and much, much, much more.

Secluded somewhere within the secret archives, the book remains closely guarded, heavily secured, and constantly supervised at all times. Classified utmost secret, thence of course, secretly ordered to be locked away. The historical manuscript allegedly entailed, several reliable and highly detailed, firsthand eyewitness accounts. The truth, is, out there. But apparently, no-one is authorized to disclose any verifications pertaining to the validity of that incredible intelligence. Rewriting actual, factual history, seems to literally, take one forever! The testamentary therein, somewhat incredulously, as one may easily imagine, vividly regales in great detail, certain circumstances, concerning one

Teeny Tiny Dragon, appropriately named Swifter, that had mysteriously arrived into this world. Said dragon, arriving out of nowhere, like magic!

We have proof. Much to our delight, thus much has been verified. Dragons are a myth no more! The entire world now knows, dragons from legends of old, of course, counting at least one, at a minimum with this miniature little one, obviously, are entirely real creatures. They once were right here. Alive and well they still dwell, somewhere out there, entirely elsewhere. The race was reported to be thriving quite well. Thriving at some ridiculously unreachable, vast, vast, vast, and even a vaster distance still. Beyond an extremely far-off place, and crazy far away. Or so they say. But at long last, the truth finally is thrust into the light.

Without a doubt, what follows is inconceivably rare. We have a newly discovered transcription, translating out for us, just a small portion of that one and only, enigmatic text. It was discovered scripted on many a golden fold. Gold folds, that spoke! Also written in script, that was in itself, pure scripted gold.

It first said. "Unfold this tale thus. In each fold is found the bending."

Researchers haven't even the slightest understanding. Not the slightest at all. Many a supposition was left to lay in silence, literally inconceivable, forever bereft, left to rest, unthought, and completely unsupported.

Never the less, this telling tale, reveals in it, so many a detail, as much could have only been gleaned from the aforementioned priceless antique tome of gold.

They call it, the book that writes itself.

1. *Into the test of time.*

My fellow travelers, consider the precious new hatchling. Destined, as the puniest dragon pup that there ever was conceived! Well, one would have to have read the scriptures to get those exact numbers. Suffice it to say, she was a really, really small dragon. In fact, the smallest of her kind, in all of the currently known histories. And on that historical note. Remember all those things we've heard about dragons in the past? Timeless fairy-tales with mighty dragons of old are found in various tales we've all been told, even up to this day. At least one ought, to have the occasion one would assume, having delighted in hearing such a thing or two. Perhaps read by a loved one, in one's own tender years of youth. Ahh yes! The classics, complete with a customary fire-breathing dragon, or perhaps, even with two! Fairy tales we, of course, have logically assumed, were nothing more than make-believe and play. Simply children's bedtime stories, albeit with fearsome dragons soaring in the sky roaring with smoke and fire. The latest rumors have it, they were probably accurate. Remarks, most likely as astonishingly accurate too. They're in one form or another, all, actually quite true.

Getting back to the little dragon. This little one in particular, honestly, was a pretty small dragon. No really, simply saying she was small, probably doesn't even come close. Not close enough to give one an accurate picture of the proper perspective needed here. See, most dragon hatchlings are about the same size as oh; let's say, a nice fat juicy apricot. Provided, that a nice fat juicy apricot, actually had wings! Why, believe it or not, when Swifter hatched was in fact, just a wee bit smaller, than a single sweet pea! Smaller, than even the cutest little sweet pea ever! Record, breaking, tiny!

This cute little legend to be, lost and alone, far from friends, far from home. Eventually, far from the itty-bitty little leather shell, she climbed out of. Swifter, always curious, always clever, always exploring, always meticulous in investigating her new forest home. Living herself a nomadic life, the once infinitesimally small speck of refined stardust, basically, camped out wherever she found herself at the time. Snuggling in somewhere new almost every night. She didn't seem to mind. As far as miniature baby dragons are concerned, the whispering woods, most pleasantly, were most accommodating. To this day, overstuffed and chock full of the most excellent, most cozy, and most comfortable kinds, of completely acceptable accommodations. Discreet and private. It continues to contain a plethora of perfectly proportional pocketry. That is Teeny Tiny Dragon size, secret little hidey holes. At present, the new hatchling simply left her shell behind. Having never felt the need, she never looked back. That day, just a little bit past four full moons ago. Swifter simply discarded it as so much unnecessary baggage. As it was no longer of any useful purpose to her anyway. Ironically, her shell still remains undiscovered and intact. Rumored to somehow have transmuted into a curl of pure solid gold. Paradoxically, how this fact can already be known? Well, no-one really knows. At the very least, they ain't saying.

Day by day, night by night, Swifter's intuitive mind, instinctually allowing her, very rapidly one might add, to become one with the forest life. For her, it was simply second nature, as it were. Naturally, Swifter found a great many new experiences. Discovering tasty treasures, finding feasts very fine, fast fellowships, and a few future best friends forever. Some, even pass the test of time. Apparently, that in itself, was the most challenging test of them all.

She saw vast varieties of forest-dwelling denizens. She had a really great time. Taking her sweet time, meeting critters and creatures, gentle and kind, virtually of each and every single kind. The histories go on to say, on the dragon's fifth day, she met up with some really pretty pixies whilst soaring on high. Off and about, soaring fast, she shot right past the last stroke of midnight...

All right. For the love of literature! Who wrote this?

So... Getting back to the pup. Somewhile somewhere, shortly after dusk. She meandered far; she meandered wide. Thence flying very deep. Flying deep into the night. Sunset had long since slipped away. Beyond the distant horizon, it dimmed, dipping low. Twilight fell, faded, and slept. The nightfall, on the other hand, was very much wide awake. Thus, the Teeny Tiny Dragon, had her very first, girl's night out. Thenceforth, Swifter shook her tiny shiny hiney. She smiled wide, pleased to meet, some really sweet, crystal clear, and effervescent sprites! Their aromatic Chieftain, Bubble Up the third, was soaring on high, as he passed her by. Also, on that refreshingly crisp, and clear night. In due time she saw, white-tailed buck deer, munching on clover. Red-tailed hawk, sittin on a limb. Chubby old groundhog. Croakin bullfrog. One arm on the wind.

She even once saw a Unicorn! Well, hold up. There are no such things as Unicorns. Those, are pure fantasies. Maybe a great big goat, but nothing resembling a horse you see. For now, let's just get straight back to the fairytale.

Well, we suppose... One ought to have a fair warning though...

When travelers collide, the ancient and the new. They'll give it their all. They'll even add in a few. Have all things thoroughly mixed, thence, fix it to brew. Here's the hard part. Willingly suspend any disbelief. Watch, and you just might see, all sorts of the most magical of mischief, that is most certain, most inevitably, quite assured to ensue.

Hold on to your hat ladies and gents! And do please, grab yourself a seat. Now would be a good time to grab some popcorn. And, maybe a tissue. Now just sit right back and you'll hear a tale. Behold! A tale in the telling as never before told! The legend of a waif, a whisper, and a warlock's world.

This is where her journey begins.

Enter the dragon. "Sniff. Sniff, sniff." Sniffed the tiniest dragon's nose. "Num, num, num." The itty-bitty dragon hummed. From somewhere near, one may suppose, that super sensitive nose, suddenly sensing a most marvelous aroma. Sensing lots, and lots, of somethings. They were there somewhere, everywhere that she sniffed! And they all, smelled really, really good. Swifter couldn't wait to see everything else, that dwelt, within the halls of the Whispering Woods. Wait... Let's have the first of those rewinding thingies. Unless that's already occurred. Making this one, the second, or perhaps, the third? That's becoming increasingly difficult to decipher. Never the less. Fictional time dilations are not all that difficult. Happens all the time. On that, one, may rest assured.

Back in time, one more time. Before it was now. Back when it was then. That was when, into this world, the tiny dragon came in. About a month before day one, she was there, alone in her shell. Yet she knew not where she was, nor from where it was, from that whence she had come. Swifter was well aware, entangled as she was tucked in there, she simply must find a way to pry herself out. Eventually, Swifter found herself emerging into an entirely new somewhere. Wherever that somewhere may be at the moment? Utterly irrelevant. Instincts just told her to make a hole. One should know, she simply had to go. Well, it was as good a day for moving away, at least as good a day as any other moving away day. The baby dragon worked mighty hard and freed herself from her snug little leather shell. It had been tightly entangled under many folded layers of Illuminatious ether. Untethering oneself after teleportation from each of the eight higher dimensions really takes some doing, just to get it straight. Seriously, that took more than a minute. Space is really bent and twisted you see. Well, Swifter was only a pup, and, she was the runt of the litter to boot. She most certainly had her work cut out for herself. She chewed and she chewed, nonstop, twenty-four days, twenty-four nights.

Once free from that endless array of entangles inside her ovoidal travel case, the adorable new hatchling slowly scanned her new surroundings. She squinted her grey eyes. The light was so bright. It hurt her eyes. They quickly adjusted to the light. Changing and shifting into greens and gold. Her pupils shone bright, shimmering twin slivers, of pale blue light. She twitched her wee nose and flicked out her long-forked tongue, its lavender tips, all waving up and down with excitement. Hungry, she tasted the air. It was as if she could smell the sweet blackberries actually calling to her, just waiting, ready to harvest. "Fresh sustenance," they seemed to say. Those fat, juicy, plump, glistening, grenade globs were most abundant. The sweet blackberries were all over the place! They covered the prickly briar patch by the millions!

List in the midst of her meal, Swifter spied the good postman, Norm. Norm loved being the postal carrier in his neck of the woods. The hardworking butterfly was fluttering by, a few parcels in hand. "Hello!" The polite postman smiled as he flapped past. Himself, firmly flapping away in full flight. Smiling sweetly, she waved back. Just then something whispered, from somewhere in her gut. "Up honey! It's easy. You can do that! Wanna fly?" Swifter sensed a strange feeling, an instinct, a visceral vibe. Encouragement so distinct. It tingled discreet, from somewhere deep, deep down inside.

Copying the mechanics of the postman flapping past, she jumped up and flew, just that fast. Gently flapping away on her flame like, wispy little wings. Teeny Tiny Dragon's first flight? What else? Off to her first breakfast, she went. Into the prickly briar patch, she lept. But of course, following her wee twitching nose. Barely out from her shell, a mere twenty-four seconds after she had just emerged. A new record! One that might never, ever get broken.

Somehow, she felt these instinctual assurances in her gut. "You got this." Her innards seemed to say. She felt ready to rock and roll into this strange, enormous, yet beautiful world. Day one... Berry patch decimation... Out freaking standing! The birth a tiny, but mighty, little dragon's legacy. At the time Swifter of course, in regards to her ability let alone origin, had not the slightest inkling. Imagine what she thought. A puny new hatchling dragon pup, having no heads up whatsoever. As one may imagine it didn't take long, until all this new stuff, everywhere, had her feeling something strange, something new. Concern and worry.

The Teeny Tiny Dragon slowly sat herself down. Thenceforth, she worried to no end. "What was she? Where was she? Who was she? Why was she here, all alone?" Poor little thing. She had no idea what this world had in store. Swifter was in a near panic. Concern and worry put on a suit and tie. Another feeling covered over the first. Swifter was becoming afraid. She felt full of fear. The wee dragon pup started trembling. She was on the verge of crying. Glistening tears, threatening to fall from her tiny shiny eyes, any second. "Swifter honey. Shh, shh, shh. Be still girl." Something inside made tiny tickles, that felt like giggles. "Just what, is that?" She wondered again. Was her belly actually whispering? Swifter heard something that felt like a quiver, coming from her liver. And, she was immediately still. "That'll do dragon, that'll do." It seemed to say. Swifter relaxed. She felt calmed. Still, the dragon hatchling really had no way to know that she was being helped, watched over, loved, and utterly adored.

"Hi, little one. Good girl Swifter. Yes, you are. Good Swifter. Best dragon ever!" Mother Earth, singing from her very core, lovingly cooed straight through Swifter's liver. Soothing vibrations and harmonic insights tingled inside, speaking directly to the tender teensy heart, of the Teeny Tiny Dragon. Swifter sensed a song being sung. It sounded like love.

Gaïa sang softly. She sang sweetly. "Yummy yummies honey. The sun's on. Breakfast is berry good baby." Swifter felt it safe to eat the berries. She felt safe for that matter. The dragon thus munched, dining on the tasty and ever plentiful blackberries. Now somehow, without a worry in the world.

In due time she'll discover she was a very special, one time and one time only, one of a kind, long distance Traveler. The distance she traveled defies all logic and reason. A first in the universe, never before attempted, multi-dimensional transference. Everything about her and her arrival, defines her as unique. Very special, by any standard, indeed.

Don't be fooled by her size. This puny one is born powerful you see. Even where they're from, dragons usually can't fly as hatchlings. Most, not even attempting the shortest of trial flights until they reach at least, their first year or so. But this unique one, created by the real magic somewhere past the way far-out zone, was blessed at birth. She held a unique chemistry, one might say. But Swifter could do far more than simply fly, on her very first day. It seems mighty and comes in very tiny, very shiny, and very pretty packages. The tiniest dragon ever was designed to be self-sufficient from the get. She was sent to do a specific job, all by herself. No other dragons came with her. There wasn't any room. They simply couldn't fit. Even though they wished they could've. It goes without saying, she really was quite far from their would-be assistance, let alone any guidance. The baby dragon was on her own, all alone.

There must be another way! How to teach her what she needs to know, in order for her to grow, into a proper young dragon? So, the Powers that be which made her able to fly the very second that she hatched. Upgrading an intentional insurance policy, those very same powers that be, made darn sure as well, this amazing pup with her very first breath of air, could do nearly anything that a full-grown dragon could do. "Perhaps more, maybe?" One might ask. Oh yes! That, and then some! She only needed a guardian. No, wait, a mentor.

Now, where were we? That's right. The blackberries obviously must come first. Thenceforth, to have an extended walk about. Or fly about? Or look about? Not sure about the nomenclature. It was about then the wind began picking up. All throughout the Whispering Woods there came a wonderful whistling, whistling with the breeze. The tune rose high, a restless rumble, slowly rising, from the tall, tall trees. Floating, lofting, lilting. Easily, the tune was carried on a soft gentle breeze. Carried softly aloft, most merrily, the wind did sing.

"Oh ho. Oh ho! There you go. There you go. What riches we have, with friends like these!

So go. So go! Then you'll know! Then you'll know! What is this, that a warlock needs?"

This was nothing new really. Even the altogether boring old rocks would sing along, from time to time. Swifter couldn't help herself. She involuntarily chirped along with the song. Singing while swinging through the tall swaying trees. Just beginning her life, she had grown accustomed to her exploring the forest neighborhoods daily. She liked the trees. She liked the birds and the bees. She liked those things that sing, those things like these, that called her mountains their home. She really liked being Swifter. Well, because she was, you know, simply Swifter, also, ironically swifter, than everything. That is, if one gathers the inference. Well into her fourth month of life, she was well fed, well cared for, well nurtured, and well, unknowingly led forward by something other than her wee twitching nose.

On one fine sunny day, Swifter was happily exploring as usual. Flying basically, just for the fun of flight. Simply winging it freestyle, having herself an absolute blast, blasting herself, all throughout her overgrown forest. She was zagging, she was zipping. In the light fantastic, she was tripping. Headset on her way to visit with some new friends of hers. A family of those speedy, little Lightship Hummingbirds. Far, far, up the hill they lived. Practically living on the edge of the world. Their miniature nests were well hidden. Tucked away, high up an old maple tree. It grew right next to a decrepit log cabin. The cabin, more of a rundown hunter's shack really, was home for this one truly ancient wizard. Two travelers, destined to be the best of friends.

Thoroughly enjoying the day, taking her time, she casually flew, meandering wide. Flying very deep into the woods. Going ever deeper and deeper up the mountainside. Swifter even took some time out to play with her friend, Drooble the wildcat for over an hour. He never saw anything quite so quick. He tried hard to catch her. He tried hard just to touch her. He tried really hard to trap her. He tried, and he tried, and he tried. Drooble eventually just gave up with all that chasing her around. With a tired plop, he flopped himself down, falling fast asleep, exhausted on the ground. Thenceforth, Swifter chased and raced a rather handsome young dragonfly. The baby dragon, smiling hugely as she passed him by, flying upside-down, and in reverse none the less! He tried, but he couldn't catch her. The young dragonfly's cheeks blushed a dark ruby red. He shyly smiled back. With just a touch of extra thrust, quickly she left him in a glittering cloud, of her golden dragon dust.

The little dragon seemed to get herself just a little tuckered out. So, she thence took herself, a little well-earned break. Thus, parking her carcass down and having a private peek, past a parcel of partially purple, partially pink, pretty painted petunias. Swifter rested up, watching some hardworking garden gnomes planting fresh veggies. It seems there were quite a few of the farmer's borrowed tools laying scattered haphazardly around. Some found their way home. Others obviously did not. The gnomes sang a song together. "Seeds in the ground, water all around." The short stout gnomes, sporting caps of red, all hummed along together, sowing seeds with their song. "Wait!" The seeds they just planted, mysteriously sprouted in mere seconds! "Ooh! Ohh!" Swifter whispered low. Intrigued, she spied a bit longer, hovering ever so quietly. Nothing new. Nothing to see. What else to do? Where else to be? She thence drifted off discretely. Eventually leaving the gnomes, to their enigmatic chores. She passed by a nebula of nymphs, six super slippery salamanders, and one, Lesser Isaac newt on a pond. Several of them critters splashed unabashed, congregating together, enjoying the weather. Living that teenage dream, playfully swimming circles around the slow-moving stream.

A short while later...

She was nearing the hummingbird's home. When something strange grabbed her attention. "What, was, that?" Swifter swiveled her spikey head and paused. She froze still in the air, hovering motionless, listening. The very moment she arrived, she heard and felt a strange buzzing. Coming strangely enough, from not too far away. It was ever so faintly emitted by a soft-spoken, thin sheet of glass. The glass was one of Ancient Traveler's bed chamber windows. Swifter's liver whispered low. "Silicates & Sorceries!" It quivered quietly so. The glass mysteriously spoke, as if by magic!

Swifter gingerly floated closer, altering her appearance to mimic the little green birds. She was sipping nectar, just like them. She was hovering, exactly like them. She was zipping around, a picture-perfect copy of them! They were gathered near a group of pretty, blood-red, handcrafted glass flowers. Those, grew strangely enough, barely hanging on a prayer from the eves. Rather convenient, so blooming close. That is, being directly in front of the very said vibrating window.

Swifter continued dropping more than a few eves. Rock steady, continued she, hovering herself closer, all while sipping some small sweet sips, from some of the blood-red blooms. Contained inside, they simply had the grandest nectar around. "Yummy, num, num.", says she. She buzzed about, decidedly hiding right in plain sight. Right out in the open where the hummingbirds had previously shown her.

About her, the hummingbirds were quick indeed. Half a dozen of those pearl-esque emeralds, wild with wings ablur, chaotically buzzed about the crystal blossoms. Intense little airborne acrobats, they were too. All hovering, zipping, levitating around. Six seriously sharp flying darts, flittering, and weaving. Each one, deftly jockeying for position. The Alpha big boys, but of course, bogarting the best all to themselves.

The young dragon saw an old grey-haired man inside the cabin. He was seated behind the glass, quietly reading a book to himself. Swifter was positively hypnotized. She cautiously hovered over another bloom, slowly leaning her earbuds just a bit closer. They flushed a deep dark iridescent blue. Flashing with each sound that came from the window.

Oh my! She truly was a most vivid creation. A flying spectrum of many brilliant lights. She could even change her colors whenever she wanted. The remarkable talent, giving her the perfect camouflage. That, allowed her becoming for all intents and purposes, a perfect little hummingbird. Hold on. Back the truck up. Why must purposes be intensive, anyway? Just saying.

As we were. There she was, so beautifully tailored. Her enchanted garments, making for a fine sublime plumage. The little dragon glowing gorgeous greens, remarkable reds, gleaming golds, and brilliant blues. Today she was just another beautiful baby bird.

The Teeny Tiny Dragon's set of cobalt blue earbuds tickled her wee spiky head. Swifter heard, and felt, the man speak. The window vibrated again. "Manisfestician Oblivious. Alpha meets Omega." His countenance had a pleasant enough aura. His voice was rather soothing too. All calm, like that lady's voice that distinctly whispered under her liver. But more manly.

The baby dragon heard the glass barely moving. Clear as crystal, it said, invisibly so, what the warlock read. "Harmony thought and deed. Cause no harm." He left off. "If these halls could talk," the warlock thought. Using his calloused old finger, he continued writing as he read out softly. "Humanity has barely begun to walk. They are the youngest of all, save one. As reflections made in fashion as us, thus, lacking our complexity. Does not the view from a mirror, no matter how magnificent, pale in comparison to its originator? None need fear, nor want, nor worry. May they be made in our likeness. Let us see the light, through eyes like these." The book thence flared into a circus of activities. Shimmering, shifting, shining, showing a jolly green dragon strolling like a queen, prancing through a rowdy crowd of rambunctious merrymakers, having themselves, a royal hoedown on the page. They played joyful music. They danced, laughed, and made merry. Bonfire and all!

The glass tingled once more as the wizard spoke anew. "Eldest and Youngest Travelers to date." Thenceforth the book started glowing a pale aqua blue. It showed an elderly grey-haired gentleman, much like himself. Same long grey braided beard. Same old grey floppy hat. Same gentle hand, gently petting Drooble, his friend, the same young wildcat. It was in reality, actually his cabin. The old sage lived there. Quietly tucked away above a burbling stream and completely surrounded by very dense, amazingly pristine forests. One could easily tell why. Built half way up the mountains, more than three-quarters of a century ago. Peaceful, private, and serene. Same as always, with a breathtakingly beautiful view too. Ancient Traveler drew a heart around the cabin with his gnarled-up fingertip. Not being able to help herself, Gaïa blushed a deep dark red. The sky everywhere immediately shifted three shades closer to twilight. Global temperatures rose 3.14159265 degrees. The world became just a touch warmer than usual that night.

"How is he doing that?" Swifter was beside herself with wonder and amazement! Here was a real Warlock, flesh and blood. Just as real as anything else she might see! The spellbinding sorcerer, simply sitting in the warm sunshine, reading his runes, writing his magic! "Incredible!" His calloused old finger moved softly over the cracked yellow pages. Scribbles just appeared, out of nowhere. That calloused old finger, mysteriously, was actually writing those strange runes! The antique archmage, happy as a lark, grinning huge as he hummed and mumbled on. His old wizard beard braids jumped and pranced! They dangled, and they danced. They tripped, they skipped, all over the page. With long legs hanging down, a lively marionette danced on the puppeteer's, private paper stage. He stopped, licking his fingertip and placing it on the book's upper right-hand corner. It was said in that very moment, the old man himself, turned another page. One Teeny Tiny Dragon, being completely and utterly enthralled, smiled ever wider and wider! She saw grand drawings magically appear on the page. The wizard of words wrote and spoke once more.

Thenceforth as he read, into a quick improvisation, they immediately went. Amazingly, his words turned into colorful sketches and beautifully rendered pictures. Those fantastic drawings actually moved and came alive! The tiny dragon squealed! "Likey, likey." Swifter could tell the crafty Conjurer was enchanting the book! He was making sounds come to life, endorsing them magically to the paper.

She was very curious. She liked the old grizzled wizard. She liked books. She really liked magic. And magic? Why it was everywhere. Swifter spied, eves dropping a bit longer on Ancient Traveler. The grey old wizard didn't even notice her in the slightest.

She decided the old Sorcerer needs a friend. Tomorrow, she shall visit him again. Now she was getting a bit tired. Her belly, now full of sweet nectar, was asking, "Now where to catch a nap?" Her little mind was thinking about finding a nice soft bed. It was getting near sunset. Flying by the porch, she spied an oval rug made of hand-braided cloth strips, conveniently laying by the door. It looked sufficient. It looked warm and dry. "That'll do." Swifter thought to herself.

With help from her gut, the brave but not foolish dragon, silently waited for the wizard, and, more importantly for his dog to go to bed. See, the man's dog had caught her sent, chuffing and woofing for a short time before he finally went to sleep at Traveler's feet. She felt it wise to wait upon the morrow to say hello. Safety first, don't you know? Not much long after, she discretely curled up in camo. She turned her little night light off. No need to advertise. Soon, she was lost in a dreamland.

The heavens above beamed down with adoration at the cutest little thing ever! The Grand Composer was surely smiling upon all those in, and about, the Whispering Woods that night. Somewhere out there, a lone hoot owl sounded off. "Whoot hoo! Whoot, whoot hoo!"

Venus, Mars, and Mercury, happened to be passing by. All marveling at what they saw. She truly was like no other. A masterpiece. Not one of them could recall seeing anything simply so fantastic. Ever!

Gaïa smiled. She felt proud. Her young dragon pup was now ready to be placed in good hands. Kind, calloused, ancient hands of the original Traveler. Mother Earth was swelling with some immense pride. That night, all her ocean tides certainly rose, to all-time highs.

So opens a new chapter. A story of hope, epic courage, and blind faith.

Rest assured. You ain't seen nothing yet!"

2. A Teeny Tiny Dragon

Perched on Ancient Traveler's finger, was a young dragon hatchling, no bigger than a mouse. Glimmering golden scales covered its lilliputian body. It began scurrying over the old man's hand, playfully flapping its wee wispy wings. A huge grin spread wide across Ancient Traveler's face, as he couldn't mask his giddiness. This was a real dragon, flesh, and blood! Far too young to maintain flight, but real. Just as real as anything else one might see. Oh, it seems dragons don't really breathe fire. Not sure if that's a pity or a good thing.

There was a knock at the cabin door. His dog went crazy, all barking and jumping at the door. The tiny dragon, frantically leaping from his hand, scurried along one of the wooden rafters exposed above. Traveler rose from his chair, slowly crossing a dusty worn wooden floor. He opened the door, grinning a giddy, gap-toothed smile. The walking antique greeted a beautiful lady visitor. As far as he was concerned, this was getting even better.

His unexpected lady visitor was holding a fluffy grey kitten. The fuzzy little creature lay, tail curled around its pink spotted nose, tucked in the crook of an arm, snoozing contently, feeling quite secure in the warm folds of her blouse. Well, the dog hadn't stopped its racket, which thence awoke said baby kitty. Thusly, sending her into a frightful panic. Now she was all hissing and clawing at the poor lady's arm.

Meanwhile, the shocked tiny dragon scampered for dear life, hurriedly skittering up the beams. Teeny Tiny Dragon, urgently attempting to squeeze itself into a thin crevice, strategically located along one of the hand-peeled timbers.

Let's see... Dog's tail wagging something fierce... Kitty clawing arm of pretty lady... A tiny dragon hiding in a makeshift lair... Albeit really small, but a fine lair none the less. One with quarters sufficient, enabling a wonderfully courageous little dragon, ample room to stand, executing an about-face, bootstrapped. Its minuscule frame boldly blocked the entrance.

The stalwart defender poked its spikey head out of the crevice. Soft lamplight reflected off her teensy eyes, two pale orbs of green and gold. Her thin wee pupils were bluer than

29

the bluest sky's. Those dancing wee pupils, now fully fixated on the man's boisterous hound.

Roundabout then was when the man finally barked at the dog. "Zeus!" Traveler's voice was loud but not unkind. He continued talking to the dog. "Wanna say hi? Go show her some love. Be nice buddy. Aww, good boy. Best dog ever." With that, Zeus jumped up, both front paws pushing on the woman's chest barking even louder, nearly sending her sprawling on the porch!

The kitty, now in full-fledged survival mode, hissed with all the fury 2.4 ounces of baby kitty could do. Poor thing was frightened out of her senses. The tiny dragon just looked down unmoving, except for her keen little eyes. Those, ineffably darting back and forth, meticulously taking in every detail. Occasionally her ears would fan open revealing deep blue patches of fine feathered scales. The pint-sized pup virtually disappeared, high in the lofty shadows. The woman lifted up the kitty, right hand under its soft white belly, while she stroked the dog's neck with her other. "All right.... All right.... Get down.... I love you too.... Down boy.... Sit!" The dog licked her cheek, quit barking, and obeyed. He sat down, tail thumping loudly on the porch. Zeus smiled his best, I'm a good dog smile, big wet pink tongue hanging out, panting happily.

Eleana came in the doorway pulling teensy weensie needle claws from her blouse. "Owie, owie, owie!" With a flump, she plopped down on a red leather couch, unfurling a billowing dust cloud across the room. Gentle hands soothed the kitty, getting her to purr once more. The little kitten curled up on her lap, thence returning to her nap.

Zeus of course, couldn't let another critter get more loving than he got. Thus, the mutt walked in and thrust his insistent muzzle under the woman's hand. The stubborn hound seemed intent on having his chin rest on top of the fluffy kitty's back. Gracie really didn't seem to mind. The little kitten, surprisingly, purred even louder. The woman petted the purring kitty with her left hand, and her other softly scratched the dog's soft ears. By this time, Ancient Traveler had closed the door and sat in his chair once more. Teeny Tiny Dragon decided their lady visitor needed to be petting it as well. The stealthy dragon pup crept carefully and quietly.

The little dragon had moved soundlessly down the wall, crossing the floor unseen. It sure surprised Eleana. It was pushing its spiked little head betwixt the lady's hand and the dog's head and kitty be damned. Smiling wide Ancient

Traveler was simply beside himself with wonder and amazement. The baby dragon began to chirp, keeping rhythm with the purring kitty and the dog's wagging tail, which of course, was banging away rapturously.

To her credit, Eleana took all this in stride. She coolly held her composure, hardly able to contain her excitement. "What on earth? Why, you beautiful little thing! Oh my God! You're so tiny. And, you're cute, cute, cute!" Awestruck, she softly stroked the brazen dragon's body, head to tail. Acting as though having a miniature dragon pup use her hand as it's personal scratching post was a perfectly normal, ordinary every day thing.

Really quite shameless of dragons. That is; they're very demanding of attention. They're particularly jealous of any other pets, yet at the same time quite accepting of the master's animals. Dragons behave themselves and are easily trained as well. They do get somewhat jumpy around loud or sudden noises. In that respect, they might flee or find a place to take cover. Given time and loving patience they're able to understand short commands, highly intelligent creatures, perhaps a bit more so than even the cleverest of dogs.

Ancient Traveler called out, "Come here Swifter." Holding out his right index finger in an inviting perching position, just in front of his nose. "Tik, tik, tik!" Clicking his tongue, the old wizard beckoned the little dragon to him. The Teeny Tiny Dragon craned its neck as if contemplating going.

Eleana began to ask questions. "Where did you get him?... Do they breathe fire? How old is it?.. Are they always that small?... Are there more? How come it's tame and not wild?... Is it poisonous? Do they bite?... Can it fly?"

She lifted the itty-bitty beast in her palm.

With that, the micro raptor leaped through the air, flashing its wings fiercely in a short flight. "I'll be damned." Uttered Traveler. "First off, not sure it's him. I'm pretty sure it's her. Just can't tell, a gut feeling I suppose. Secondly, up till this morning, I thought they were only in fairytale stories. It's strange appearance, is obviously proof they're not just a fabrication born of fantasy. Oh, it's undoubtedly true. They're certainly real enough. It's just that, they're not from here, not anymore anyway."

The tiny dragon landed on his finger. The dog licked the lady's hand as she subconsciously toyed with his ear. The kitten purred steadily, still quite happy to stay curled up on her lap.

"It was sleeping on my porch when I let Zeus out this morning. Good Lord! You should've seen the ruckus. Zeus went over and sniffed at it, just lying there. I thought for all the world it was dead. But the critter woke up and ran up my leg, squeaking, and chirping. Boy! Can it ever move? I tried to grab it running over my belly but it was too quick. Beats all I've ever seen, and I've seen a few things. Difficult to see, this little dragon is. Before I could stop it, the damn thing buried itself in my pocket. It wouldn't come out for hours. Zeus kept sniffing at it, chuffing his disapproval.

I tried to carefully pry the creature from my pocket, but it sunk its claws firmly into my shirt. Didn't wanna hurt the poor thing so I quit messing with it. Kinda scared me a little. Didn't wanna get bit. You know? I put the dog outside and just talked softly to it. The wee thing slowly came out all by itself. Ain't bit me yet, don't think it's venomous. That's the word you're looking for. She's really smart. She understands, I think she does anyway. She likes me. There must be others. You know? Gotta be... Right? Anyway, I've never heard anything about them being seen here, let alone in this era. Maybe legends from millions of years ago talk of similar creatures, but those were much, much, larger. I've read that the species; Draconia, Sentientio, and Behemothian, still thrive far away. But it doesn't make any sense. You probably wouldn't believe how far they say either. I wonder why this little one showed now, napping at my doorstep?"

Flapping her brilliant wings, the dragon started playfully wrestling with his thumb. The baby dragon had four legs, and a long slender tail with a pair of pointy fins at the end. Twin copper-hued rows of ridges ran the length of her spine. Her wings, sprouted from an articulated pair of jet-black vesicles just the back of her shoulders. Strong gossamer thin membranes ran down to her rear legs, spreading between her outstretched wing fingers. Each wing's standard issue, was a full set of itty-bitty razor-sharp claws, equipping those surprisingly firm fingers. As a hatchling, they're roughly the same size as an average hen's chick. But this unusually diminutive dragon could sleep in a thimble!

Her claws lightly grasped Traveler's thumb while the tiny dragon pretended to bite his knuckle. The wary wizard spoke curiously, speaking directly to the dragon. "What about that kitten my dear? Where did you get that? It's really cute." She then turned to look at him, her ear buds flashing cobalt. (The dragon not the kitty).

Seemingly caught with her hand in the proverbial cookie jar, Eleana lowered her head looking down at the kitty. Flashing her eyelashes innocently, a big smile crossed her face. Like a rogue, she spoke boldly. "I stole her from that

Oger at the bottom of the mountain." Rubbing her fingers gently between the kitten's ears, she continued. "There are about fifteen more kittens under his shack. She let me pick her up and instantly started purring. The others all ran away. I'm going to keep her and I'm going to call her Gracie. I didn't see that Oger though. Thank the Gods!"

Traveler wrinkled up his nose. "Good Lord! Think that you should have?" Eleana frowned at that, looking more than a bit injured. The playful prestidigitator simply winked at her and smiled. He lifted his hands and giggled grinning. "Easy girl, don't go do no crazy voodoo magic on me. That's all we need now, dueling wizards! But Burley, I suppose he's alright. It's his rundown lair that needs some thinking bout. Real nasty things also live near that place. One may never know, some hungry wild cougar or those icky little goblins maybe, even a ghostly barrow wight or a mob of pixie forest sprites could getcha!"

A serious look thence crossed his face. Speaking to the dragon again, he turned the pint-sized thing around to face him. "Please, keep your distance from that place. You know it ain't safe." Eleana sighed, rolling her eyes. "Whatever. He'll never know. How could he even tell she was gone? He won't care at all. He doesn't need her. He'll never give her any love ever, but I will.!" With that, she scruffed up the kitten's neck if only to emphasize her point. Gracie stretched out her paws, completely helpless under the woman's long-nailed fingers. The kitten leaned into each caress purring loudly, shamelessly demanding more. "See. She, loves, me." Little needle claws, pawing away, as Gracie began kneading on her knee.

Swifter took notice of her hands roughly scruffing up the kitty's neck. In a flash, she bolted off Traveler's finger! With one fluid motion, she jumped, flapped, and landed on Eleana's hand without making a sound. Thence the plucky young pup proceeded to worm her way under Ellie's fingers, resting herself on Gracie's shoulder. Zeus, fascinated by the sudden movements, sat back on his haunches, watching, woofing, chuffing, and barking. He sniffed at the new visitors. Thenceforth, he sniffed them once again, just to make sure. He thought they smelled nice enough. The curious old dog, keeping his big brown eyes squarely locked on, watching most intensely, set his mind on following the show, very, very close.

"Wow!" Eleana whispered softly. Gracie turned her head completely around, nose to nose with Swifter. Slowly lifting her hand, Eleana squealed with excitement! "Look! Look! Oh, would you just look at them!" Swifter sniffed at Gracie. Gracie growled, puffing up her fur, and arching her back. Zeus chuffed. Swifter chirped. The dragon's eyes locked firmly onto Gracie's. Transfixed, the kitty was mesmerized! She froze still, left front paw, curled and at the ready. Sweet slow chirps came from Swifter. Her pupils, like liquid slivers of the palest blue water, widened and narrowed. Her shining eyes shimmered soft, lit up by minuscule flames. The lantern's glow had jumped into, and onto, her entirely captivating gaze. Tiny shining eyes made for perfect mirrors in miniature, faithfully reflecting, two fine flickering flames. The spellbinding dragon seemed to have a hypnotic effect on the kitty. Gracie reached out one paw slowly towards Swifter. Swifter, mirroring her movements, lifted her wing. The tiny dragon moved her sleek body, swaying left and right, holding her wing steady, nearly touching Gracie's paw. Ripples of fractal iridescence began rolling down Swifter's body. Thousands of scales, shimmering like a living kaleidoscope, pulsed in time with her spellbinding dance. The Teeny Tiny Dragon could glow with light! She made the room brighten significantly. Ten thousand score, brilliantly bright stars, and more, suddenly lit up the cabin! Cast about everywhere, shined countless colored rays of crystal-like beams. Streaking through the cabin's dusty air, tiny galaxies danced everywhere. Eleana sucked in a slow whistling breath. "Wheeeeeuuuuuuweee!" The lights instantly went out.

Swifter cocked her head around searching for this new sound. That's when Gracie shot her paw out to pap the distracted dragon. It appears the spell was broken. In the instant Gracie made her lightning-fast move, Swifter was quicker, impossibly quick. Her wings switched places. Her sleek body swung away from the paw, letting it pass to her side. This reminded the old sage of that fabled matador bull fighting faring from far distant shored. "Toro! Toro!" The masses would have roared! "Olay! Olay! Olay!"

The tiny dragon flipped her bright wing at Gracie's paw, striking sharply, snapping back fully unfurled. Gracie launched at her wing, pouncing with both paws. Swifter practically blinked from the getting squished place, to the not getting squished place, right next to Gracie's shoulders. Pap pap! Gracie then received two paps from Swifter, both softer than goose down, striking quicker than a viper. Teeny Tiny Dragon deftly delivers a left and a right to the kitty.

Ancient Traveler giggled, snorting without intent. Eleana giggled too. "Oh my god! They're playing! That's the cutest thing ever." Swifter leaped at Gracie's throat. POP! The air made a noise like when pulling your finger out of your mouth. The dragon attacked. Swifter moved so fast she blipped out of eyesight, reappearing under Gracie's chin. Ancient Traveler saw something Elena and Gracie couldn't.

Swifter wasn't just quick, she disappeared and then reappeared instantly. Traveler wondered if she actually teleported.

Swifter, grabbing four wee handfuls of fur, teased the kitty. The baby dragon began flashing her wings playfully left and right. Gracie danced in circles on her hind legs, front paws boxing, obviously delighted by her new friend's talented performance. The kitty tumbled back off the lady's lap, landing her bottom abruptly on the floor. Teeny Tiny Dragon had taken down Goliath. Eleana and Ancient Traveler rolled with laughter till their bellies ached and tears threatened to fall.

Kitten and dragon both began rolling across the hardwood. Zeus got up dancing in circles around the brawlers, egging them on with his chuffing and barking. This activity continued on for a couple hours. Over every inch of the floor. On each step of the ladder leading up to the loft. Across the loft. On the sofa. Under the sofa. Zeus barking his constant critique, hot on their heels. Kitty paws, just flailing feverishly in attempts to trap the bright little dragon. But to no avail. No matter what Gracie did, she simply could not catch her. Swifter was wickedly fast. Gracie tried to pin her down, over and over, until weariness invaded her body.

Eventually, all three took a nap on the couch. Zeus was the first to succumb. He finally climbed up on the couch, laying down, head nestled on the arm rest. Gracie curiously followed afterward. Purring, she pawed and kneaded at the old dog's neck. Zeus kept right on sleeping. Swifter watched and waited from the floor. As soon as Gracie lay down tucked under the dog's chin, she hopped across the room, up the couch, over the dog, and burrowed herself under the kitten's chin. Zeus snored. Gracie purred. Swifter squeaked. All were sound asleep.

"Ellie, won't you stay for supper?" Asked Ancient Traveler in hushed tones. "It's getting pretty late. You oughta stay for the night." Eleana stood up slowly stretching her arms. Yawning wide, she whispered low. "Uh-huh, yeah. I was thinking about that. It's almost dark now, I was gonna ask." Ancient Traveler replied.

"Yup. I was hoping you would, milady. I got some fresh rabbit and a bit of tater. How 'bout some rabbit stew?" "Sounds great!" Eleana quietly whispered again. "Do you have anything else like celery or carrots? How about garlic?" Traveler got up. Eleana followed him to his kitchen pantry. "Yeah, I got all that. We got plenty of fixings. I'll get right on it." "They're out cold. Why are we still whispering?" She cut him off speaking softly, reaching past him grabbing a bag of potatoes, thenceforth brushing him aside and shooing him out. "All right old man. You go rest in your chair. I'll cook tonight, but you're going to do the dishes, not me." The tired old traveler raised his hands in mock surrender. "OK fine! As you wish my dear."

Ancient Traveler sat watching her prepare supper. He drifted from watching her, to watching the sleeping trio. The Teeny Tiny Dragon began to glow, ever slightly so. The fluffy kitty purred in her sleep. Her neck looked for all the world like some silver-lined grey puffy clouds. Backlit softly, puffs of fine fur, caressed an extraordinary in truth, miniature midnight moon. Zeus curled his tail around the pair, ever so gently embracing Gracie and Swifter. Sniffing them both before himself, drifting soundly back to sleep.

In no time, Eleana whipped up a delicious dinner of rabbit stew. Complete with homemade biscuits and sweet wild honey. The two enjoyed the company even more so than their most delicious meal. The stew was simply perfect.

After a fine meal and the dishes had been gathered up, Eleana followed suit with the critters. Carefully sitting down, she cozied up to Zeus. Gently petting the dog's thick red and yellow fur, she rested her sleepy ole head on his big broad shoulders. Wrapping one arm around his back, the other she tucked between her knees. Laying back on her side she curled up and began snoring softly. The old dog sniffed for a bit at Ellie's neck, thence once again he drifted back off to his slumber. In tandem, returning to his snoring right along with hers. Ancient Traveler paused his dishwashing long enough to fetch a blanket from his bed-chamber. He lovingly tucked the cutest little quartet in for the night. He softly kissed Ellie and Zeus on the head before he left. After a short while, the dishes were finally finished. He left them to dry till morning …

Not wanting to disturb the others, Ancient Traveler slowly crisscrossed a squeaking hardwood floor, blowing out a pair of flickering lanterns as he did so. Surrounded by sudden moonlight and shadows, he quietly and carefully crept on his way.

Entering his bed chamber, the tired ancient one pulled a fading dark brown curtain across the opening. Outside, a countless array of sparkling stars framed a waxing half-moon. Gleaming bright, Luna smiled wide, looking as though she was looking right at the old worn-out wizard. Puffs of fine grey cloud, lined with a silver hue, brushed softly against, the magnificent midnight moon. The weary ole wizard smiled wide. Taking a moment, he stretched out slowly, yawning a great yawn that came from deep inside.

Tough and rough old fingers, scratching his rough enough, wiry old whiskers. The archaic archmage, just for a moment, just stood still. Peaceful and serene. Standing simply spellbound, as he always had, gazing and daydreaming, lost in awe upon the splendor of it all. Time and time again, he thought of them as priceless jewels, vast riches without end! Each is perfectly set by the Master Craftsman's hand. Magnificently displayed and forever resting upon an endless purple mantle! The master magician mused aloud. "Indeed, these must be the Creator's trove of treasure! An undercover treasure, that one may only discover, during the dark of night."

The half-asleep sorcerer was illuminated by the pale glow of moonlight and stars. He got undressed down to his skivvies, crawled into bed, and slid under a thick patchwork quilt. Curling his arm under a cool pillow, the old grey-haired sage closed his eyes. Whispering a prayer to the universe, he fell asleep. Many a thank you on his breath, having many more, welling in his heart.

Looking upon them slumbering contently away, Celeste lovingly stretched out, curling herself around, and ever so gently embracing the quaintest quintet of quietly sleeping travelers. Luna smiled hugely. Watching spellbound, the Cosmos continued shining down on their dreamscapes. Even the Great Expanse couldn't mask her giddiness! Down there, those were the real priceless gems. Although they, of course, had no way of knowing that. Spinning and grinning, all of creation was astronomically filled with wonder and amazement. As always, masterfully setting ever more and more priceless gems, throughout the whole of the night.

Who knows what the morrow may bring.

Sleep thee well my fellow traveler. Sleep thee well.

3. Calm Before the Storm.

Good Morrows.

Ancient Traveler awoke to the sound of bacon frying over a crackling fire. The smell of fresh coffee floated in the air. It's enticing aroma, silently compelling him to rise. Contrary to popularly held opinion, the best part of waking up is actually waking up. But along those lines, the coffee this morning did smell particularly good. He stretched out, wriggling the quilt off his legs. Putting on the same worn trousers he wore the day before, he grabbed some fresh socks, his boots, and a heavy cotton shirt. Thence he gave the shirt a quick sniff. Checking if it was safe to wear. It smelled of smoke and earth, but it didn't stink yet. Thenceforth slipping the garment on, he thought aloud. "Ahem. Hmmmm... Close enough." "Hoot-hooo, hoot-hooo!" Calling unusually early, an urgent hoot owl thence sounded off from somewhere deep within the woods.

Stretching his arms and yawning wide, Traveler brushed his heavy curtain aside. To the east, a beautiful orange sunrise had already awakened the magnificent palisades full of rugged and rocky, fir-rimmed peaks. Sol was steadily rising over the valley's far side, shining bright, filling the cabin, with her soft warm light. "Whoot whoot whoo! Hoot-hooo! Hoot-hooo!" Louder and bolder still sang out that hoot owl again. Traveler thence stepped into the cathedral, a name he occasionally uses for his living room/front entry. Its high-pitched ceiling, always hanging thick with long-neglected cobwebs, vaguely resembled ruined stone temples built many ages ago.

Ever the thoughtful soul was Eleana, humming happily in the sanctuary. Cheerfully busy at the woodstove, pouring out two hot cups of dark steaming brew, she kindly handed one over to him. Taking the freshly brewed coffee in one hand, his other, firmly gripped his boots and socks. The antiquated archmage moved fluidly, dramatically, and intentionally. Quite majestically, his magnificence, grandly bowing low. The high-spirited sorcerer, never spilling a drop. All this, including his coffee, smoothly swinging out to the side, graceful pinkie, of course, extended over theatrically. Bowing low, Ancient Traveler cheerfully intoned. "Well, Good morrow. And a hearty thanks to you, milady." She loved to hear him talk like that. So sweet she thought. Well, old-fashioned play acting certainly was in his nature.

Ellie laughed as she watched his extravagant performance. She smiled sweetly. "I put Zeus and Gracie outside. Please don't let them back in. I wanna finish breakfast first." Ancient Traveler was already headed to the door, steaming coffee in hand. The old wizard just loved to sit on his porch early in the morning, checking out and listening to the overgrown forest. Relaxing for a while as one takes their leisure, really does a wizard well. Inquiring as he stopped, Traveler swiveled his head towards Eleana. "Have you seen Swifter?"

With piping hot coffee pausing at her lips, Eleana gently blew on the brew. "Oh yeah. She's under the rafters, right there." Eleana pointed her left index finger at the spot the baby dragon set up her camp. "Well, it seems she found her lair," Traveler remarked. "Did she get scared?" He asked, concern showing over his brow. "No. Nothing like that. She was hunting a moth. That's where she went to eat it after she caught it. Wow! Is she ever fast! I can see how she got her name." Eleana sounded proud.

Ancient Traveler took a small sip from his cup, looking up. "Say. That's really good." The grateful sage piped out, swallowing the dark brew with a deep rumble of satisfaction, flowing naturally through his voice. Traveler craned his neck around until he spotted Swifter. Just the tip of her tail gave her away. It was behind some cobwebs, scarcely visible. She was fanning it around all lazily, half hidden behind the shadows. Her two teensy tail fins, dancing, coiling, lollygagging, swishing about to and fro. Eventually, following the little dragon, herself, scarcely showing behind her otherwise astonishingly concealed frame.

Traveler turned around reaching for the brass door knob. Well, the clever conjurer was clumsily fumbling with the knob, the same hand, still clutching, his boots and socks. He opened the door really, really, slowly. The old wizard, strategically placed his left foot low, in the air, and at the ready.

When cracks of daylight widened in the jamb, Gracie immediately flashed through! She deftly avoided his clumsy blocking tactics, her little lithe body, smoothly contorting beneath his bare foot. She was in the kitchen before he could even register the tickle of fur! "Hey!" Dropping his socks and boots, he snatched her up by the scruff of her neck. Blink and you'll miss it quick Traveler, nimbly placing her outside on the porch in a flash! Impressive! Most, impressive. The surprisingly swift sorcerer, never spilling a drop!

Thenceforth taking full advantage of the situation, Zeus abruptly brushed him aside as he forced his way past. The wizard wobbled, rolling on his heels off balance. Therefore, spilling half his coffee down his trousers. Ancient Traveler quickly grabbed the dog's collar with his free hand. "The old man has still got it, eh?" He bragged to Zeus.

The stubborn old dog slowly turned around, dropping his head in shame. Sheepishly, he walked back out. The upset mutt sat down as Traveler let go of his collar, whimpering and looking, truly pathetic. His big sad brown eyes pleaded with the man. "Please let me join you. Please. Please. Please let me in." A soft beard of white hairs quivering, up and down on his sad little chin. "Knock it off! Ya big baby." The sage scolded sternly. "You're fine outside. See. I'm going out too. Silly dog." With a gentle pat on the head, Ancient Traveler closed the door. Zeus smiled huge, panting happily. His big pink tongue curled down and out. The happy old dog began giving the much older Traveler, a rather solid thrashing from his rather solid, thick bushy tail. The stubborn dog finally sat down. Traveler smiled. "Good dog." He said to Zeus. "Thump, thump, thump." Went the dog's tail.

Having himself a nice big tasty gulp from his steaming hot cup of joe, Ancient Traveler stepped off the porch, fixin to sit. Suddenly, a flurry of feathers and squawking makes this terrible din in the morning air. A startling flush of flapping wings abruptly brushed his face. It appears he had inadvertently stepped on Matilda! His pet hen.

Matilda, profusely squalling, took to the air flapping frantically. The indignant hen launched herself over his broke down half rotten fence. Well, she felt down right put out. And quite understandably so.

Having hot coffee fill his nose, scald his throat and splash down his face, Traveler bent over and spat. "Sorry, Tilly." The confounded conjurer coughed out clouds of piping-hot steam. Certified fair market, one hundred percent pure organic, piping hot steam. It, steadily escaped into the sunrise, stinging and hissing, off his rather upset, and java-moistened countenance. The rarely rattled wizard stiffly wiped his drenched mustache whiskers, scrunched up his soggy beard braids, and took aim. With a gap-toothed grimace growling low, he snarled, "Let's dance." Well, both hostile aircraft and a waltz, oughta be well led. In full surround, Traveler could almost hear the dueling banjoes, pleasantly picking through his head.

Playfully, the wizard thenceforth locked one calloused index finger on his rapidly fleeing target. The timeless trickster thus opened fire. Suddenly, cracking cannons sounded off with the outgoing anti-aircraft artillery. The dodgy old mage had let fly, five mini munitions. "Bawk Bawk Bawk Bawk Bawk!" Ancient Traveler was feeling positively mischievous, having himself a few playful potshots at the swiftly retreating hen. The prehistoric old prestidigitator was engagingly accurate too. Steaming hot tracers went streaking out, right at her six. Explosions in the sky, popped like puffed-up pincushions! Daringly close behind Matilda, burst itty-bitty clouds, of fresh live grounds! Nipping at her tail feathers, the ordnance composed, of five tiny rows, of bold and black, dark Sumatran flack!

"Well. Good morrow to you too Matilda!" He boomed, mirthfully coughing the words out. Taking one last careful sip of coffee, thenceforth finishing his cup. "Oh! Man! That really was good!" Traveler slurped it down with genuine satisfaction as he sat. His old achy frame complained grunting, whining. Grunting and whining, from several, random new locations. "Hang it all! Man, I'm getting old!" Traveler whined a bit as well, plunking both damp derriere and now empty cup, firmly on the porch. Zeus licked at the scruffy old wizard's, unkempt whiskered cheek. The happy dog wagged his tail, yet again. "Good dog."

Now seated on the porch, the venerable vagabond from days long gone, once again, as usual, was simply taking his sweet time. The ancient to the extreme wizard was internally still. His mind was as clear as the clean morning air. Stretching backward to retrieve his boots and socks, he found himself, wriggling most awkwardly. The winsome wizard wriggled away, eventually getting around to putting on his socks and boots. He was in reality, lost in a world of his own just peacefully daydreaming. Somewhere in mid-boot, the serene sage paused. Traveler heard the hoot owl hooting again. "Whoot-hoo! Whoot hoot hoo!" The wise old wizard had learned to listen to the woods long ago. More intense than ever, the owl was saying a storm was about to appear. He quickly tied up his laces.

"Oh really? Do tell. Didn't you have it a wee bit wrong the last time?" Ancient Traveler asked of the owl. Who of course withdrew from providing any answer. Standing up he turned around, stretching. "Snap, Crackle, Pop!" the man's noisy old body grumbled some more, griping something fierce, as he moved for the door. "Yup, I think you're right. It's gonna rain for sure." He grumbled as well, stiffly walking back into the cabin. Ever the responsible sorcerer, Ancient Traveler uncharacteristically found himself remembering, therefore quickly closing the door, before Zeus could attempt any more of his, unruly uninvited incursions.

Zeus barked. Zeus grumped. Zeus chuffed. The old dog felt tricked. He felt cheated. Zeus scratched and pawed on the door. He wailed. "I want in. Please let me in." Zeus whined and whimpered and whined some more. Complaining several times, before laying at the door. The little kitten, on the other hand, had other things in mind. Gracie froze still. In stealth mode, she was now stalking an unsuspecting leaf. The leaf rolled over teasing and taunting the kitty, suspiciously tumbling in close. Temptingly, tumbling much too close. "Meow!" The fuzzy kitty pounced. Glancing out the window, the timeless Traveler found himself chuckling aloud. "Ooh. You almost had it. You gotta be quicker than that. ..."

Inside the cabin, a hot breakfast awaited him freshly set on the table. Eleana was sitting at the table, already in the middle of her meal. She was obviously delighted to dine with Swifter. Before her, a miniature legend from antiquity was actually sitting on the edge of her plate. "This is so cool!" Eleana thought aloud. Swifter looked at her and smiled.

The Teeny Tiny Dragon sat with her beautiful body shimmering bright, on an ornately engraved silver spoon, utilizing a piece of toast as her makeshift table. The precious gem of a thing copied Eleana's etiquettes most meticulously. With the purpose of mind, she closely watched her every move. Because she knew that Ellie knew what a lady would do. The baby dragon held her food most daintily. Her hands, each smaller than a dandelion's parachute, exhibited a surprising amount of dexterity. Swifter had her wings of gossamer folded back, transformed into a soft cowl of magenta, crimson, and black. It flowed past her shoulders, cascading elegantly down her back. An adorably adorned young lady dragon, munched most happily, albeit somewhat noisily, on a fresh hot crisp, of nice tasty bacon. Her elegant royal highness, seated upon her own, ninety-nine and forty-four one-hundredths percent pure, imperial sterling throne.

"Come on and eat hon, it's getting cold." Eleana invited the wizard, pointing towards his plate. The meal consisted of crisply fried potatoes, and two eggs, their broken yellow yolks seeping towards several slices of juicy bacon. Pale toasted bread, with a fat pad of butter, rounded off breakfast. A jar of sweet orange marmalade was sitting next to an invitingly fresh, full cup of steaming hot coffee. The breakfast looked truly amazing. "Oh, that smells so good." Traveler heartily declared. As Traveler sat down, he quietly said thanks to his creator. He was hungry and he really loved marmalade.

After an exceptional breakfast, Ancient Traveler got up and headed back out. "That was great." He said while grabbing a musty dusty jacket, hanging off a rather untrustworthy rusty bent nail. "I'll be back after the chores." He put it on and closed the door. "Let's go, boy." Zeus got up following with his whole body wriggling excitedly. The wind had begun picking up. Gusts were scattering leaves about his porch. His forest started whispering, and trees began to groan. Another hoot owl warned. "Hoo hoo! Hoo hoo!" Apparently, this really was going to be one doozy of a storm.

As his lady visitor tidied up the cabin, Traveler went to his love and called it work. He quickly fed the fat furry bunnies, Rockchester, Emerson, and Montaray. The wizard, double checking cages, locking doors, and refreshing water trays. He fed Matilda and Gracie, giving them a kettle of water to share. He put the kettle where it could catch falling rainwater under the eaves. He fed Zeus, giving him the last of the rabbit stew and fresh water in his bowls. Zeus gobbled his breakfast, shoving his bowl under the house as a result. His wagging tail doggedly followed in hot pursuit.

The mindful magician decided he ought to go fetch up some dry firewood. Crossing a few steps to the woodshed, Traveler opened the pair of swinging doors. They gave out a mournfully aching creak, old rusting hinges, complaining profusely! "Crik, Crik, Carikeek!" Swifter copied, sort of. She had blinked outdoors, bobbing like a robin. Making her way, lightly bouncing over the dirt path to the shed. The curious little dragon expertly scrambled up the closest swinging door and firmly perched herself on top. With her strong haunches ready, the dragon raised up her wings. Buffeted by gusting winds, her delicate wings were all ablur, constantly fluttering about. Keeping her wee little body, rock steady. Weaving for stability, a wee baby dragon walked on the wind.

"Ahh well." The wishful wizard mumbled aloud, a bit bummed out. Peering inside, this particular morning, his woodshed was completely empty. Oh sure, there were some scattered twigs and blackberry starts were there. But only one piece of cordwood, not yet split, remained inside. This simply would not do. "Well, crap." Traveler softly cursed. Swifter popped her jaws and whipped her teeny tail, "Cawap!" She cried. Her tail cracked high. Her body flashed a glimmering green light. "What's that you say?" Traveler turned looking curiously at Swifter. The marvelously magic miniature dragon rang out loud. "Cawap, Cawap, Cawap!" Eerily followed suit by the whispering woods, echoing her mimicry, hauntingly faint. "Wap, Wap, Wap..." A chorus of teeny tiny curses, reverberating behind her, came calling back, coursing through the leaves.

The surprised sorcerer pointed his crusty dusty calloused finger, at the teetering little dragon. "Hey, there honey. What's that? No cursing now sweetie." The old sage nodded his head to Swifter with a firm grin. His fat bushy brow, inferred discretion. Thence, kindly winking one discretionary inferred, bright hazel eye. Swifter bowed her head to Ancient Traveler, chirping nonstop. The precocious baby dragon, was obviously, quite pleased with herself. "Well, Cawap!" Teased Traveler as he laughed out loud.

Thenceforth the sorcerer picked up an axe propped in the corner. He called out loud. "Zeus!" His old dog came out from under the cabin's timber-braced floor with his entire body wagging. "You too Swifter. Let's go for a bit of a walk, shall we? We're gonna get us something to burn, keep us nice and cozy tonight. Wanna go?"

Swifter dropped off the door, letting her outstretched wings catch the wind. Soaring up like a kite, she lifted smoothly skyward. Having her fluttering sails fully unfurled, a lovely little longship, flashing and gleaming, swiftly set off sailing ever higher aloft.

The Teeny Tiny Dragon, quite unknowingly, was sailing toward some dark and not-too-distant clouds. Ahead of her loomed an ever-approaching grey wall of gloom. Obscured behind that most gloomy wall, advanced rank, after rank, of mighty thunderheads. The Gods of thunder approach. Amassing with them, a million crackling minions. Lighting cracks the sky. Boom, Boom, Boom! It makes you weak. Not too far away, the heavens boiled.

"Oh yeah, almost forgot. Think I just might need this." Ancient Traveler paused, snapping his fingers. "Pow!" The codgerous old conjurer quickly snatched a grey pointy hat, magically flopping out of thin air. Quintessential and certainly quite essential, it suddenly materialized, smartly dispatched by a cordial butterfly postman. The currier, pressingly making his rounds. His bright flittering wings, fluttered the postman past in a hurry. "Always forgetting something sir." Flapping away, he chided captain obvious. Or perhaps oblivious? That possibly or would probably depend upon one's perspective.

Well anyway, time was of the essence, as they say. About a fifteen-minute hike brought the trio to a large clearing. Dropping through a lush valley they passed by several severed cedar stumps. Stumps, of monstrous proportions. Men had harvested this forest many decades ago. Huge cedar trees became huge cedar stumps. Scores were left behind, rimming the tree line. Many, well over seven meters in circumference. Most had long since turned into small rotted hills. All were completely covered, practically encased with needle-thorned, thick-caned, and twisted-up blackberry vines. Carefully zigzagging between the dense briars, moving along the edge of the tall, tall trees, Traveler stopped next to a sizeable dead-standing alder. The careful conjurer eyeballed his intended target intensely. Once it was a Titan amongst the others. It would've taken at least three men to reach around the dead tree. "Alder makes a pretty good fire." He told Zeus. Zeus agreed. He wagged his tail. Swifter agreed. She wagged her tail. Her grin gleamed. Her sharp eyes shone brightly. "Cawap!" She cussed. Landing on a blackberry, tiny maw wide open, she plunged her face down. Tail fins intermittently followed, delving deep into the heart of her prey. A ravenous dragon's liver quivered within, "Let the eviscerating begin!" Swifter soon became a purple-sticky mess. Zeus wandered around, sniffing at everything.

The talented Traveler could've harnessed something much more magical to do the work for him, but Ancient Traveler, with a few reservations, intentionally chose otherwise. He instead spent half the day chopping at the huge tree in the time-honored tradition of older men. Fell it by chopping out wedge-shaped cuts, first on one side, then the other. Chip by chip, chunk by chunk, chop by chop. All by hand. It was tedious work. Soon, the old conjurer was wheezing for air. Occasionally Swifter, slathered with slick purple gore, lifted her head from her latest oozing and dripping victim. The Teeny Tiny Dragon, simply checked out the noises, seeing what the wizard was up to. Reluctantly, Ancient Traveler went back to his chores.

Swifter thence, scrambled up a fat green leaf, having emerged out of the sundered heart of another hapless meal. She propped herself up and used her slender forked tongue to clean her glistening purple body. Rain fell about them, creating little craters in the dirt. Just a few noisy drops, as they were. But they spoke volumes. "Pip pip, pap, pip pat pip."

Traveler cautioned Swifter and Zeus, "Listen. Ominous harbingers, they forewarn of things to come. Mark my words." Swifter resumed her cleaning. Zeus smiled, oblivious. The sky was getting pretty dark, pretty quick. Thick clouds, billowing in the form of misshapen grey gargoyles, now, fully blotting out the sun. There was an insistent wailing in the air. All the forest hissed in the wind, moaning, creaking, groaning. Leaves and branches flew by, apparently of their own accord. Lighting cracked high overhead from way past the ridge. The thunder boomed, rolling on a month of Sundays. Swifter, anxiously twitched her tiny spikey head about, her dark cobalt ear buds fanning out nervously. The tree began to creak and groan as Traveler hacked the final felling blow. He hollered, "Timber! Hey Zeus! Move buddy." It came down screaming, with that unmistakable, inherently alarming cry, that comes only from cracking timber. Crunching, shrieking, cracking. Tearing apart, it tumbled over at the hinge. The dry trunk snapped loudly, soundly hitting the earth with a meaty, "THA WHUMP!" The ground shook violently. Zeus jumped and yelped. Dry branches exploded, sending shrapnel shards of deadwood, dangerously close to them all. Alarmingly, much too close. "POP!" Swifter immediately vanished, creating that finger-pop noise again. For an instant, the tiny dragon left behind a violet silhouette of the faintest blackberry mist, barely hanging. An ultra-fine purple juice sculpture, a tiny picture-perfect still shot, somehow hung silently for just a split second. Momentarily, it held motionless in the air, exactly where, the tiny dragon had recently been sitting. Before it too disappeared, forthwith becoming scattered, summarily obliterated by the wind. "Just a vapor in the wind. Aren't we all?" Said the weary old wizard. Zeus barked. He growled at the fallen tree. The dog bit into a broken branch. Picking It up, he carried it for a bit, pacing around, walking in circles, looking for the perfect spot to lie down. Finally, he did lie down. Thence, cleverly using his front paws to hold onto said chewing stick, he thenceforth, happily chewed bits and pieces and chunks off of the end. Zeus was really happy. He wagged his tail. The wizard was really anxious. He wiped his brow. "Wow! I guess that settles it then." Staring off towards the cabin, Traveler looked concerned. Something told him she was there. He could sense tension, but he was certain Swifter was now at home, safe, probably playing with Eleana.

The rest of the afternoon Traveler methodically chopped and split firewood from the dry dead tree. The wise ole Warlock thought to himself, "Best to split up the whole thing. As, he was already here, axe in hand." Most of the day had gone by. Traveler stopped and listened. Big fat raindrops plopped, plinking on leaves and drumming up songs as old as time itself. "Pip, pip pap, pop." He could hear a double entendre from the percutaneous music. More drumming came in. Distant thunder rumbled, the lingering thunderclap, growling low, slowly rolling overhead. The earth thrummed and shook with the intense report.

The wheezing old wizard hollered over the whipped-up wind. "Right on, thank you. This oughta burn great." A salutation for the fallen Titan. Metaphorically not literally. "Burn great, great, great ..." A snarky reply resounded, sharply echoing back from the shaded hillsides. Ancient

Traveler patted Zeus on his back. Zeus barked at the woods. They barked back. Swifter was still missing in action. Worry, gnawing at his innards, made the old wizard hasten his chores.

The rain started falling steadily. It was nearly dark, an hour or so till sunset. This had really taken much longer than Ancient Traveler wished. He thought, "Oh well. Work is honestly, more rewarding than any sorcery. But maybe next time, I think I'll call on the postman. Norm wouldn't mind. Certainly, not too much." Taking what he could, he gathered an armload of wood, piece by piece. Leaving the rest behind for a later time, he wobbled his way back to the cabin. "Oh, ow!" Ancient Traveler's back burned. His tired arms were aching, attempting to keep his fingers locked around a wet bundle of wood. A bundle, that alarmingly threatened to tumble away at any given second.

Now the rain was seriously falling hard. With his nose down, and wagging tail up, Zeus wobbled all the way home. The wet, worn-out wizard, wearily followed. Half exhausted, he too, wobbled all the way home as well. "Click, click, clack! Creak, crack, snap!" Even Traveler's tired ole bones, groaning all by themselves now, were openly complaining, grunting, griping, winging. "Thank, the Gods!" The soggy sorcerer smiled. Up ahead, he caught sight of a yellow lantern's steadfast glow. It had been set out on the front porch. On this stormy night, that guiding light, was shimmering bright, leading them both safely home through this most dreary of downpours.

Thoughtfully, somebody left a light on. That really means a lot, for anyone getting themselves caught, out in the dank and the dark.

Could this possibly be the end? We think not.

Something was obviously missing here. There were certain questions yet to be asked. Unasked questions that needed certain answers. Tonight, the approach of dawn, creeps along, arduously slow for this most unusual group of travelers. It seems that they were all in for an unusually long, and rather arduous night. Except for Zeus, Gracie, and the fat furry bunnies. They were all, actually quite okay with it. At least, they got to sleep like babes tonight.

Sweet dreams fellow traveler.

4. *Matilda's Rainstorm.*

They call me Swifter.

Matilda was missing in action. Fierce forks of lightning were flashing close by. Thumping away in the sky, thunder was rumbling, rolling like giant-sized, gigantic kettle drums. A heartbeat before lightning soundly took out the mighty and once majestic Sherwood, and yes, the maple tree by the window has a name. At least, it did. Really not sure about how it would currently choose to identify itself. More than likely, it switched from Sherwood to Firewood. Just before the electrifying lightning strike, Swifter had picked up Matilda's faint cry. Far and away, too faint for the others to hear. Even far too faint for Zeus. Young little Swifter had made up her mind. She was going to go help.

Determined, Swifter popped outside, racing off in full flight. She headed towards Matilda's call. A gentle rain was slicing around her sleek body as she flew headlong into the fray. Flapping with all her might, Swifter had materialized herself in the air, a good twenty meters away from the cabin. The truly concerned Teeny Tiny Dragon, selflessly started streaking forward. Swifter's afterburners accelerating her supremely sleek fuselage, instantaneously, pushing all her state-of-the-art giros, far and away past the Engineer's, theoretical redline. Thus, exceeding her expected output, unexpectedly quick. Unexpectedly quick, indeed. Behind her, two bright blue cones of wickedly hot plasma flared to life, screeching out her dual vesicles of jet black. Pha-Boom! A shockwave collapsed, clapping loudly behind. The air gave way, snapping out a fine vaporized delta. It crisply fanned behind the baby dragon's ballistically induced wake.

Lightning in the sky, overhead crackled high. Matilda squawked with high anxiety. She was very far away. Rain began to fall in earnest. The audacious aeronaut flicked out her slender forked tongue. She cried out. "Ma-till-e!" Swifter could sense that the lost hen was terrified. "That way!" Her taste buds said. Instinctively empathetic, Swifter instantly warped over a quarter mile farther from home.

She re-materialized at full throttle. Much to her dismay, the pup was entirely unaware of the countless inherit dangers. Imagine the perils, an untrained hatchling pup teleporting at speed! Let alone, attempting such a great distance in one so young as she. Henceforth, a very hard lesson instantly was learned. Impacting a sheet of driven rain, a fierce blast of steam painfully exploded in her face. Scalding hot water was suddenly forced into her tiny eyes. They hurt, stinging intensely. She was severely stunned. She had never been hit by anything. Ever! Scorching vapors choked her itty-bitty gasping lungs.

Raindrop artillery assaulted her, attacking from on high. Repeatedly, dive-bombing her relentlessly! Pummeled as never before, Swifter was getting beaten down. The stunned young pup found herself suddenly plummeting from the sky. Her stunned body tumbled head over teakettle, crashing savagely, utterly uncontrollably, spinning the out-of-control little dragon, haphazardly through the trees. Branches were indifferently slapping, unapologetically smacking, at her dazed and confused drenched wee little body. Brave young Swifter reacted quickly. All thirty, of her beyond razor-sharp micro claws, ripped desperately at the flora rushing past. Her claws finally struck a limb. With all the might she could muster, she raked her strong talons firmly into the branch, thankfully arresting her fall. Trembling, shaking, precariously perched was the baby dragon, desperately grasping for dear life. Swifter was gasping desperately for her breath, gratefully gulping in great gasps of the fresh clean air, feeling it cool her lungs. She felt a little lightheaded, just a bit dizzy. Something wasn't right. The stunned little thing tried looking through the tempest, but her stinging eyes were nearly swollen shut! Only black, indistinct, grey blotchy nothings could she see. Swifter was completely blind. She was also, completely confused. "Who turned out the lights?" She couldn't understand where her vision had gone. Her eyesight, once, was keener than an eagle's. But all she could see now were imperceptible fuzzy shadows and darkness. An encompassing darkness that encased, enveloped, and endlessly surrounded, the terrified tiny dragon. Swifter was truly afraid. But what could she do now? Should she simply break down and cry? Her gut told her, she would be fine. There is nothing new in the night. Even though her entire frame was trembling, achy, and shaky, frightened Swifter thought herself a thought. "Don't let fear stop you." The lion-hearted pup boldly declared to the world. "I got this!" Gaïa wept with pride and admiration. She just couldn't help herself. She cried out buckets and buckets of compassion, and torrential rain poured over the mountain that night. It had to be done eventually anyway. Her wild flowers could certainly use some hydration.

Meanwhile, inside their deluxe apartment in the sky, magical miracles are about to mysteriously manifest themselves in the midst of mayhem. Unceremoniously picking themselves up off the mirror-like marble floor, a pair of shocked and surprised bright blue sprites, instantly became a pair of sprawled-out, skip-skipping, bright blue beanbags. The completely unexpected impact and subsequent free fall chaotically tossed and scattered everything throughout the entire palace. Including, the pair of normally very bright, identical twin siblings. Thus-forth, the sprawled-out sprites, therefore, collectively composed themselves, calmly addressing the situation. Roland and Winfred Immediately jumped into action. Roland began, "It appears we've lost the screens." Winfred responded matter of factly," Yes, as a matter of fact, her receptors have temporarily lost the feed. We can get the pictures back with a little Ambrosia, or, a lot of time." Roland suggested, "Let's see if we can help her in the interim. Please, do be a good man and turn on the deep field sensors if you will. I'll retune her audio collection arrays. She's going to want to be aware of her surroundings."

The twins thence started messing with some antiquated machinery. Thenceforth rusted cogs, gears, belts, and pulleys, momentarily screamed as they began rotating. The loud machinery continued squeaking. Snapping, hissing, and popping intermittently thereafter. An enormous set of polished brass pipes boldly began producing a most pleasant sound. Powerful puffs of steam came bursting out, rising higher and higher under the vaulted ceilings. Pleasantly, whistling away with magical melodious, harmoniously haunting tones. In the background, three strong chords strumming, thence came thrumming in strong. All set, to a quite heady, rather rock-steady beat. The whole palace seemed to be singing. An entirely altogether massive gaping maw, of a gigantic antique bronze boiler, began belting, itself, entirely altogether massive big bold baritones. With precision and perfect timing, a set of polished pistons pumped and clunked, drumming a steady rhythm just like big bass drums. Subconsciously humming along, Roland busily poured over the old yellow pages of a worn user's manuscript. Always the gentleman, he politely asked his brother, "Winfred, would you please clear the screens, my good man? And be so kind as to hit the reset for us." Winfred was already readying his station for the new input. "I got this. There it is."

Painstakingly, the bright sprites toiled at their task. Slowly fine-tuning the two giant screens that now were currently frosted over. The ginormous displayers crackled hissed and blurred, having grown very dark, very dim. The reception now has little picture at all. "Soon, we'll all be able to see as she would. That is, if she were right there, at home with her kind. Roland applauded his brother, "I say ole chap, well done! We can give her the whole package. Let her observations flow directly from our ocular fields. She's already designed to handle the extra data." Winfred liked the idea. "That's brilliant!"

The miniature blue sparks worked diligently, methodically adjusting the baby dragon's extremely delicate, antique quantum machinery. Burning the midnight oil, both the figurative and the physical, until long into the night. Swifter suddenly sneezed. "Cashews!" An invisible, inconceivably thin shield of plasmatic energy, momentarily emitted out from Swifter's fine feathered scales. Her entwined sub-nano emitters flared to life, initiating rebooting after the twin's long arduous process.

Thenceforth, transpositioning any foreign quanta frequency, harmonizing anything away from and instantly around, the tiny dragon's body. Just, like, magic! Soon, she'll be able to do anything that a grown dragon could do. That is if the twins can link her core to the nearly endless possibilities of Mother Gaïa herself. If all goes well, within a few short hours, nothing could ever again touch her. Unless of course, she actually wants it too that is. She might even be able to teleport other things, like those mysteriously missing, precious pretty things. Other things, other than her pretty little, priceless precious self. Wheels and pistons chugged, churning behind the pair. Thick clouds of steam and dark smoke puffed out, swirling together high in the air. "Huzzah! Her quantum field is holding! Just don't enable the warp driver until she adjusts her incoming energy receivers." Roland could hardly wait, "She's going to experience so much! This will really enhance all her senses you know! Just think, exponential inputs, are linked to possibly infinite information. Well, this is going to be quite an interesting adventure. Let us hope she's ready. Shall we see, what twelve trillion, Quantum bits, of potential possibilities can do?" Positively giddy, Winfred was whole heartedly in agreement. "Oh, this little dragon hasn't seen anything yet!" Thence the brilliant Willowisps together as one threw her inverter's dual switches on. Electrically charged particles flooded through vaulted ceilings. With a great crackle, the palace thrummed and shook. Swifter's mind began receiving thousands upon thousands, of simultaneously overlapping inputs. Each in excess, of thirteen trillion teraflops per second!

Thus, the smallest dragon ever slowly came online. Sure, there was some minor tweaking still necessary, but the process was flowing smoothly and apparently successfully. This kind of empirical rebooting had never been attempted before. On anything, let alone the Creator's very finest. Not ever. The Grand Engineer was really impressed. The wonder wisps actually improved upon the inner workings of her Creator's, "Pièce de résistance." The newly updated young pup began sensing unexpected sensations. Swifter was picking up good vibrations.

"Ka-Boom! Boom boom. Ka-Boom! Boom boom." All around her lightning relentlessly proceeded with striking. Guttural soundings of thunder crashed throughout the entire forest. Swifter heard the thunder roll, but she couldn't see the lightning strike. "Ka-Boom! Boom boom." Matilda squawked and cackled. She was above Swifter, sheltered not too far away. The scent of her lemon balm perfume barely touched Swifter's sensitive nostrils. Matilda was close. The tiny dragon's purple-forked tongue quickly flicked out, tasting the air. Her body spun like a compass, with pointy tongue forks, pointed straight at Matilda. Fortunately, the hen was only about ten meters away. Unfortunately, she was stuck in a tree well over fifty meters higher up in the canopy. She wondered, "How on earth could she possibly ever reach her now?" Swifter yelled, for lack of any better term. "Ma! Ma! Ma-till-e!"

Sometimes things just work out. Swifter's high pitch squeals registered in Matilda's ears, who in turn, clucked hopefully. "Bawk, bawk, bawk!" "Till-e, Till-e, Till-e!" Swifter called back. Thenceforth the brave little dragon felt her way along the branch. She reached the tree's trunk, purple tongue flicking, checking her bearings. Matilda was still somewhere up in the next tree.

Completely blind, Swifter used her other senses to guide her way. She could still smell, she could still hear, she could still taste the air. Her new software, now feeding in vast amounts of alternative inputs. Swifter's massive miniature mainframe hummed in the process of updating her refined senses, bit by bit. The miraculous master engineering enabled her to entangle Euclidean processors and unprecedented quantum superiority. Her multi-dimensional, biological machinery, flawlessly operating exponentially. Incredibly, exceeding their original capacity by an impressive factor of twelve, to the incredible power of thirty trillion! Winfred exclaimed proudly, "Huzzah! We're successful old chap. She's aligned with Gaiia. And now, with us. Time for the show and some popcorn." Roland thence rang a small silver bell.

Two amazingly beautiful royal blue Djinn, each wearing pristine white cotton tunics, sporting layers, and layers of fillagree fine gossamers thenceforth appeared. A matching pair of silken blue Genies, floated smoothly in, coming from the kitchens. Both were covered head to toe with dozens upon dozens of gleaming gold bangles. Ungodly expensive, finely detailed, exquisitely crafted, blazing diamond jewels sparkled all about their strong blue bodies. They were draped with dazzling heavy chains crafted of pure shining gold. Sporting thick twisted links, coiled and clipped to dozens of fantastically crafted miniature magic charms. Each set, with the rarest yet, and even more priceless, beautifully breathtaking stones. Each Djinn carried a plain hand-painted white porcelain bowl. The bowls were filled with delicious, freshly popped sweet cream buttered, white corn kernels. They also brought in with them, just a pinch of the purest, pale pink Atlantean sea salt there is in existence. Much, much more valuable than either silver or gold, or even the Djinns' diamonds! An unbelievably rare, indulgent treat. Temptingly ready to sprinkle right on top!

Swifter the magic dragon, vaguely smelled the ghost of Tsushima, and strangely enough, a vague hint of popcorn. She shook her soaked wee head to clear the cobwebs followed, by thoroughly shaking her drenched and aching wee body.

An ultrafine mist thence exploded all around her. A rainbow spray of cast-off rainwater, brilliantly lit up, by her countless microscopic scales. Suddenly, a sparkling veil of gleaming subatomic stars, spontaneously ignited around Swifter, flaring brightly in every spectacular color, across every spectrum of light. For the slightest of moments, a molecularly thin wave of plasmatic energy, erupted briefly around the youngest dragon in history to go full-on plasmorphic.

Swifter now discretely possessed, direct access, to archaically profound powers. This surprise advance, is serious, although currently unknowledgeable, a complete game changer. She was now capable of anything, anything at all, that a full-grown dragon could do. Even though she had no way of knowing it at the time. She really didn't know, she could actually throw, super-heated plasma. Wicked hot plasma, that's even hotter than the center of the sun! Not quite breathing fire, but the effect would be quite catastrophic. Especially detrimental for any would-be target. One would say, they were having a seriously bad day! "Must say! This really was, getting even better!"

The tiny dragon, tenaciously grappling wet slippery bark, carefully crawled down the tree's trunk. Swifter was having a pretty hard go at it. Gale force gusting winds menaced, threatening to rip her away, any moment. The bark was slick and slippery. It took all she had just to hold on. Nevertheless, she was just as determined as ever to reach Matilda. When she finally did reach the ground, Swifter found herself surrounded by water pooling in deep depressions around the tree's roots. Small ponds of rainwater were blocking her path. They might have well-been oceans to the blind baby dragon. Outright resolute, Swifter adapted and groped her way around this new challenge.

"Bawk! Bawk, bawk, bawk!" Matilda gave out directions. She made, I'm up here, sounds. Around the tree, Matilda was currently taking refuge, stretched out a terrible black water ocean. Although its depth was little more than a few centimeters deep it presented many perils. Its dangerous swells were tossing and churning, wind-whipped, frothing up forebodingly. Storm waves crashed around Swifter's toes. The frightened hen was trapped, far, far up, a tall tower of swaying cedar. It's massive wooden walls, looming terribly high up from an island, securely ensconced in the center of the black stormy sea. Lightning ripped at the sky! Thunder pounded painfully in her sensitive wee ears. Swifter began blindly testing the shoreline with her wing, reaching down, and probing at the water's edge. Time and time again, she couldn't touch the bottom. She would have to swim if she wanted to reach the island. Because of the rain, Swifter couldn't fly across, she couldn't teleport, and she couldn't see.

"Buh bawk!" The hen clucked nervously. Without the slightest hesitation, Swifter courageously crawled into the water. Rain fell in buckets. It cascaded in sheets blown sideways. It pummeled the Teeny Tiny Dragon's wings and beat on her back. Swifter could not swim, but she was so light and small, surface tension supported her teensy little body. Swifter could literally, walk on water!

She was making slow and steady headway, skittering like a water skeeter. But for every little bit she gained, the wind shoved her back. It shoved her sideways. It came at her from all directions. Suddenly, a fierce gust filled her wings. Like a sailboat zooming out of control, she slammed painfully into the cedar.

Precisely at that same instant, within their luxury apartments, Roland and Winfred's popcorn spontaneously flew across their mirror-like marble floor. On the other hand, the two powerful blue Djinn simply continued shoveling coal into the blazing boiler unaffected, behaving as though nothing had ever even happened. Both the bright blue elementals laughed in unison while the twins regained their composure. "The snacks mayhaps, just a bit premature in concept?" They continued shoveling coal, laughing still, with even their featureless black eyes smiling. Themselves, peering out of another realm, faring from someplace else tangled within an even deeper dimension further within. For just a moment Swifter felt that. She faltered and froze. The surprise impact took away all her breath. Her wings ached, and her back burned. Her legs felt the bark digging into her flesh. The shocked Teeny Tiny Dragon cried out in pain. "Yee-eee-argh!" Wincing, she struggled mightily to maintain consciousness. Her head swam. "Hang on girl, we're almost up to speed." Winfred grimaced as he felt the instant deceleration. "You poor dear. Soon Gaïa can eliminate any further damage. Hold on just a bit longer girl." The Willowisp wonder twins hurriedly spun a variety of dials, shifted an array of leavers, and quickly flipped a myriad of switches on an antique mahogany switchboard. Swifter's sensitive ears heard a whisper in her skullcap. The kindest of voices clearly said, "Hang on. Hold on. You're strong. Now hurry Hon, you must move on. Go now! Be swift! There isn't any time!" Swifter shook her wee spikey head. Now, feeling a bit clearer and more determined than ever, Swifter boldly began to climb.

Rain was falling hard. The forest was getting hammered, pretty darn good by the storm. A long slender widow maker suddenly impacted the spot Swifter had just vacated. It stuck deep in the mud, thumping loudly with a sickening splat! Like a million pins thrumming, the Teeny Tiny Dragon's claws tingled intensely. Swifter felt the entire cedar vibrate, feeling every branch quivering, each needle being shaken. She even felt Matilda's clickity clackity feet, anxiously pacing, grasping for purchase on a limb somewhere high above.

Swifter painstakingly, climbed for over an hour. Doing battle with the storm's forces, she never conceded one iota. Which is actually quite some distance, considering her size. She held her ground and pressed her advance forward. Just a couple feet, only a few more steps. She thought again and again.

The plucky tiny dragon was slowly getting closer. "Till-e!" Swifter called out reassuringly, letting the hen know her rescue was well in hand. Matilda saw the teeny tiny heroine approaching from below. "Bawk! Bawk! Bawk!" Over here she called to Swifter, relief flooding her emotions. The tiny dragon touched Matilda's toes with her wing. Matilda was safe. Swifter was exhausted, but safe.

Matilda covered the soaked little dragon with her wing. The worn-out dragon, wrapped her thin frame around the hen's boney leg. "Cluck, cluck, cluck." Matilda called motherly, sitting on Swifter, her brocaded feathered skirt, snugly covered up the baby dragon. It was dry under her wing. It was warm. Blanketed by Matilda, Swifter soon regained her strength.

Swifter could sense Eleana and Ancient Traveler were worried sick. They couldn't venture out in this storm. It was far too dangerous for them to risk. They were forced to wait it out. Matilda and Swifter were on their own. If there were to be any rescue, they'll have to do it themselves.

Swifter poked her tiny spiked head out of her blankie. Matilda cocked one eye at her. Swifter chirped. The hen blinked. Matilda didn't understand. Swifter began making the magic sounds she had devoured in the library. "Prestidigitation maladroitness." Unfortunately, Matilda didn't speak magic rune sounds either. She just clucked motherly again.

Swifter had to get Matilda home, she had to get the chicken to listen to her explain. "Stalwortly venture. Harbor fortitude. Draconic desideratum origination." She outlined her plans as simply as she could express. Matilda blinked at her, just oblivious. "Buh-Bawk!" Apparently, she would have no more of it.

Trees were snapping, winds were whipping, lighting was striking, thunder was rolling, and rain was drenching the entire mountain. Eleana took a lit lantern to the kitchen window. She slid the pane open. "Swifter! Matilda!" She called out, anxiety was clearly palpable in her voice. Outside, a worried Traveler stood on the porch scanning the storm. He saw nothing but a roaring soak fest, displaying the storm's incredible power. Not a sign. No Swifter, no Matilda. Ancient Traveler felt his innards churning. He could scarcely hear Eleana's voice. It was indifferently stolen, completely whisked away by the piercing whistle of the harsh winds howl.

"Ma-till-da! Swif-ter!" Swifter heard Eleana. Over a quarter mile away, the tiny dragon's sensitive earbuds detected her voice, despite the cacophonous noises raging everywhere! Her head pointed towards the origin, purple tongue tasted, but got nothing to register. Matilda clucked, "Bawk Bawk." That was her, "I'm gonna shake all the water off my feathered body, and go to sleep." sound. Swifter held on to the hen's apron of fine fluffy feathers, firmly grasping both the literal and the audibly obvious. "Deponent comportment." Swifter suggested to Matilda, but her chicken brain couldn't get the gist of the report.

Matilda did as she forewarned. Thence, shaking the water off her body rather vigorously, fluffing proper, and side-stepping herself a bit further up the drooping bough. There was more cover here, closer to the trunk. Lighting crackled, the bolt striking a fair piece away. The peal of thunder, encouragingly tarrying several breaths, before

83

gutturally rattling across the sky. The entire cedar shook. Matilda held tightly to the limb. Her strong, long-clawed feet were engineered for exactly this very thing.

A proud mother hen tucked her new, teeny tiny, soft and shiny, beautiful baby chick in for the night. "Bawk. Mama got you, honey. Bawk. Mama got you, girl." Matilda cooed sweetly to Swifter. The exhausted baby dragon just let go, snuggling securely in the hen's downy soft bed. Swifter rolled into a ball, falling fast asleep. The wee magic dragon began to glow slightly so, slowly getting brighter, the deeper she fell into a dream. Roland and Winfred were still busy at work, literally burning the midnight oil.

Back at the cabin, Ancient Traveler slept on the couch by a cracked open window. He slept deep and restful, mouth half open. The storm finally moved on as it always will. Zeus slept on the floor next to the wizard dreaming, legs twitching, nose sniffing. Eleana slept with Gracie on her belly. She dreamed of flowering fields under the summer sun. Dreams about her mother, her daughter, her kitty, and her friends. Matilda purred in her sleep. Zeus chased after a squirrel, woofing and running while he dreamed. Traveler drooled on his pillow, comatose. He didn't dream of anything. If he weren't fast asleep, he could've seen a tiny new star, shining bright in the forest.

Way back in the backwoods, Swifter chirped, fast in a deep sound sleep. She glowed brightly, twinkling with outstanding iridescent waves. "Incantations, blessings. prestidigitation, preparations, protectorate." It seems her wings were sleep flying again. Colorful wings, brightly flaring in step, with the Teeny Tiny Dragon's, dream-induced chirping. Matilda was lit like a lantern shining through the lonesome dark. Luna passed by just before dawn. The moon, absolutely beside herself with wonder and amazement. Completely fascinated, she couldn't take her eyes off them, fully admiring the superb craftsmanship of the fantastic masterpieces. All night long, Matilda's bright beacon shone, over a quarter mile from home.

Just as it should, a new day will surely dawn. Thankfully, by the look of it, she's just around the corner. As always, the wheel in the sky keeps on turning. Once again, just as it should be.

Good night.

5. A Big Burly Ogre.

The Counting of Kittens.

Matilda was gone, missing in action. Desperate voices rang loud, searching from somewhere deep in the woods. "Swifter! Ma-til-da! Swifter!" Burley could hear the wizard's search party. They were calling for swifter and the lost hen. Unfortunately, that was precisely when the big burly Ogre was attempting to count his kittens. Suspecting one or two may have gone astray. Things got more than a little bit strange as he struggled with his count. "Ten, eleven, Tilly, twelve, thirteen, Swif-Ter!" He stopped in mid-count and thought. "Swif-ter? No... That's not right." The big brute was working hard under his apple trees amongst throngs of mewing, chewing, playful little grey kittens. Energetically enthusiastic, obviously overly acrobatic, extremely charismatic, little grey kitties they were too.

His pet heifer Bessie followed after him relentlessly. Quite hopelessly, lovesick. Much to her credit the graceful Jersey doted on and absolutely adored the slightly rough around the edges big burly Ogre. Bessie herself was always the sweetest cow. With the best of manners. The very picture of a lady. This cow in particular loved to follow him around. Flashing her long black lashes. Sashaying her wide hips. Constantly demanding petting scratching and attention. But for now, she was determined to assist him with the counting of the kitties.

Seemingly everywhere, several kittens and a few freeloading felines freely roamed the orchard with them. About them. Around them. Under them. Behind them. Three brave little kitties attempted, rather unsuccessfully, climbing over them as well. Well, one doesn't have to be a rocket scientist to get the gist of the situation here. The award-winning big, beautiful blue-ribbon bovine, really wanted to help her man. She carefully herded the mass of kittens. Inching the little hairballs slowly toward him. They, just, scattered! Unwilling to stand up and be counted. Unlike cows, kitties it seems, don't have any decent sense of order.

She thought, "Don't you know? Proper cattle, always go, where they are, supposed to go. A wise bovine follows inline." Bessie mooed. "Well, I never. At least a cow would know, what to do." Still, Bessie was unperturbed. She turned around trying to move the group again. Some kitties scattered. Some kitties did not. Some kitties climbed the ladder. Others tangled themselves in a knot. "He, he, he." Laughter fell freely from the forest canopy. Giggles wiggled in and under the bright green leaves. Kittens and kitties mewed. They tackled. They chewed. Some, diving under his shack. Others sprinted around the back. They hid in the bushes. They climbed over his fence. In turn, they chased his positively panicked hens. They raced after them, all, crazy. Just a bunch of rambunctious, feline youngsters.

Simply doing what young kittens do. Clamoring around the orchard. Having a grand time with it too! It was pure chaos, a cacophony of madness! Cute little inducers of madness, one must admit. Looking precisely like so many clones of one another. All identically cloaked, with matching grey coats of fuzzy fine fur. Thence, the big ole Ogre turning in even bigger circles, began trying his hand once again with the counting of a few kittens more. But big ole Burley's vision somehow went all blurry and hazy. He got all dizzy. They all spun around the orchard like mad whirling dervishes. All of them, again, all, crazy. That would be; Burly, Bessie, and the really rather playful cast of kitties. For a time, several even tried pouncing at a butterfly. Norm was a good man about it all. Actually, a good butterfly. But that's a matter of semantics. The playful postman was playing along by leapfrogging over a long line of furry little fuzz balls. Taking it one flap at a time.

Bessie, sashaying sideways as she both, swung both, her hips, and the rusty front gate. A firm bump from her plump rump, easily swinging it closed with a clunky clunk clank! Burly tried, "Wait! Wait! Don't forget, to latch, the gate! Like the last time." One can only guess what happened then. Big ole Bessie, the grand girthy girl, was helping get the feral pride a bit more motivated. It seemed she ended up not exactly in quite the right spot. Guess one really had to be there. Bessie, almost having them all rounded up, till she took one fateful step. One fateful step, a touch too close. "Meow!" Then off they all go. Scattering with the wind! Fleeing so. Instead of being civil again. Scooting away, their frantic little paws furiously scrambling. The panicking little kitties left little panicked-induced dust trails spreading out. Just like the spokes of an old antique wagon wheel.

The De-Vine bovine began herself, turning in a fairly wide circle. To see what was tugging from her own, fairly wide behind. A surprised Bessie jumped around, startled! Knee jerk kicking with as much kicking as any cow could possibly kick. "Moo! Moo! This, would not do!" It appears several kittens had begun playing with her long swishing tail. "Moo, moo, moo! Shoo, shoo, shoo! Moo, moo, move!" She chastised, the entire lot. One held on tight and got himself batted about like a bouncy ball on a long rubber band. Three strikes, and he was out! No need to count to ten. He knew he was done for the day. The dizzy little kitty coiled up to take a nap. Counting himself thoroughly out for the count.

Hiding forest sprites watched from behind the trees. They couldn't believe what their eyes were seeing. Mirthful giggles rose in pitch. Leaving the leaves in thorns and stitches. Pixies laughed alongside their kin, from just within, the shade of the whispering woods.

"Was this getting good? Oh my goodness! Was this ever, getting even better!"

Thenceforth, the calling searchers resumed their sounding off. With the Whispering Woods adding in the faintest of echoes to return upon the wind. "Matilda, Swifter! Tillie, Tillie, Tillie!" they called. Stubborn old Burly simply began counting his kitties again. "One Tilly, two Tilly, three Tilly, four." He had a good rhythm going. Well, for a second. "Swifter! Tillie! Tillie Tillie!" The party called out some more. "5, Tilly 6, Swifter... Oh, bother it all! No no no. Not that, either." Burly gave it a go again. He said, "Let's see. 1, 2, 3, Tillie, Swifter Tillie." The search party cut him off. Yet, again. Ever more and more laughter filtered freely from the glade.

The Whispering Woods just rolled on. "Tillie, Tillie, Tillie!" Tall fir trees chuckled in the breeze.

Giggles fell from up on high. Falling steadily from the thick green canopy. Some branches were really cracking themselves up. They were so stiff they wouldn't even begin to think about bending. They simply had to grin and bear it. Not to be outdone, the haunted hills themselves, joined in and wailed away.

The headstrong Ogre thence picked up handfuls of kittens. His cracked and dirty, scarred-up knuckles were getting stuffed. Stuffed with clawing, mewing, profusely protesting handfuls of unhappy little kittens! Burly bravely counted the writhing mass of clinging kitties. They frantically scrambled out one and all. Clawing for dear sweet liberty. "A one, and a two, and a three," says he. So far, so good.

Meanwhile, a bit further down the steep dirt road. A very curious neighbor just had to take a peek at the strange going on. A thin, old lady troll stood watching the affair as it unfolded from afar. "What was this?" She really wanted to know. Creeping, like a Golem sneaking, Trollette tiptoed. She waited and watched entranced. Dozens of kitties came storming past the onry old Ogre's split rail fence.

Bessie was utterly shocked! The graceful prize winner mooed out her urgencies. "Moo, Moo! Shoo, Shoo, Shoo! This won't do." Oh, dear! It seems Burley's mountain Momma cat had called her third cousin over for the holidays. Who in turn, of course, had brought with the entire kit and kaboodle! Now there were two score more, carbon copy fuzzy grey little kitties scrambling around. Just like all of his own little furry kitties. All were adorned with the very same coat of soft grey fur. The mighty mob of mini moppets marched on. Brazenly stampeding ahead. Fearlessly charging into a score, or more, of curious little kittens that Bessie had just lured in close. Proudly, she was sharing some of her very own locally produced farm fresh milk.

Grabbing some hairy handfuls more, Burly was sure there were surely more, fuzzy grey kittens at his door than there were just the day before. Bessie mooed. She didn't know what to do. "Shall we try it again my dear?" The Ogre, the Wizard, and the Whispering Woods somehow all said in unison. Traveler thence started up the drill once again. Followed in suit by Eleana, and par for the course, the Haunted Hills of course. Simply having to accompany the Whispering Woods with a little reverb and four-part harmony. (See? This really was, get-ting good!)

"Swif-ter! Tilly, Tilly, Tilly!" The searchers cried. Burly tried. Bessie mooed, stupefied!

"1, 2, moo, moo, moo. 3 4, count one kitty more. Moo, 5. Is this right? Moo, moo 6, Swift-ter than this. Tilly is moo moo, that. Moo, 7 moos? No, she's that mountain momma cat. Moo! Ma-til-da! 8. No wait! Might have missed one or two. Moo. Moo, moo, moo." It seems several uncounted kitties were still streaming in. Running through his gate. Despite this development, the stubborn ole Ogre was undaunted. Positively, Homeric in his efforts! You see, some Pixies and Sprites had been secretly singing along. Discretely urging them on. Don't you know? One more time, Burley tried. Alas, he never got to nine. Not like the first time. "1, 2, Moo, moo, moo. Swift-ter! Tilly, Ma-til-da! Tilly, Tilly, Tilly!" Burley, Bessie, Traveler, Eleana, scores of Sprites, packs of Pixies, all of the hills, all of the tall trees, they all, strangely sang along. Mixing up all the songs. A song was sung. The likes of which even the mountains had never heard before. "3 4, itty bitty kitties more. Tilly Swift-ter! Tilly, moo 5, moo, moo, moo!" Gracie then showed up too. She clawed and pawed at Bessie's hoof, mewing for love. Well, why not add another kitten? Oh, for heaven's above! Then the song began anew. Yet, again. The winds roared! The winds blew. The woods whispered with a haunting tune. Good Lady ole

Willow had thousands of thin skinny long limbs wiggling with the wind. Wiggling, jiggling, and giggling, most uncontrollably. Even the usually dour weeping willow could not seem to stop herself this time. Yet one more time, Burly tried. "1. Moo moo, Tilly 2. Moo moo 3 4. Hold the door. Swif-ter 5, Tilly moo 6. Swif-ter 7, count a few of them again. Tilly, Tilly, Tilly," Thence, with a wail on the wind, the Whispering Woods once more, joined back on in. "8, Moo, Moo! Tilly!... Tilly!... Tilly!... Moo Ma-Tilly!" Oh my! This excessive exercise was getting hilariously silly. Well, one hopes one can clearly see where this is all gonna go. It appears Burly certainly has his work cut out for himself this time. Maybe Bonnie can help?

But wait! We're not finished. Not even close. Wait till one sees what awaits right smack dab in the middle of the road...the fabled fairytale continues...

6. Leap of Faith.

Or if one prefers, how to fall with style for
dummies.

The dawn woke up to greet Ancient Traveler, Eleana, and Zeus, already walking towards her. She peeked over the ridge, and there they were. Obviously, looking for something, and urgently so. Sol took it upon herself to shine a bit brighter, burning stronger to better light the way.

Matilda tenderly roused her little chick, gently nudging the sleeping baby dragon with her beak. Swifter yawned and stretched out. Blinking her somewhat tender and swollen eyes, she saw that the world had remained black and blurry. Very black, and very blurry. Swifter was still blind. She couldn't see anything. Gingerly climbing, she felt her way to Matilda's three-lobed comb, centered on the top of the hen's head.

"Ma, Ma-Till-E!" Swifter petted Matilda's neck. "Bawk." The hen came back. Suggesting, "Swifter, buckle up!" Without any hesitation, Matilda simply took off. Suddenly jostled, Winfred and Roland moved quickly, securely fastening their brand-spanking new, fancy five-point safety harnesses. "Descending delights!" Swifter roared, feeling the wind's undeniable pull on her wings! Giving a great lift, to body spirit, and soul.

Fearlessly, Matilda abruptly launched herself from the cedar's sheltering arms. The blind baby dragon found herself suddenly flying. They were brazenly barnstorming, thrashing through the thick trees. The tiny dragon had the utmost faith in her unusual aero plane's unique abilities. Without a single worry in the world, Swifter settled in her cockpit, just above and between, Matilda's strong flapping wings.

Swifter really wanted to fly, her high spirits, willing them up. "Oh, just a bit more. Come on Tillie, just a little bit more..." She held on, all six sets of her strong tiny talons, gripping firm. The tiny dragon and the squawking hen flew something around seven-hundred-fifty meters together in total distance. Pretty impressive for a chicken.

For a few moments, Swifter was flying by the seat of her pants. She leaned weaved and bobbed past branches brambles and twigs. Sensing all the whooshing forest greens, wildly rushing past her sensitive wide-open ears, the draconic aviator banked hard, twisting tight. Swifter sent Matilda insanely spinning through the thick branches, with a seriously full-on feather clenching, innards churning, series of branch kissing, branch clinging, high screaming corkscrews! Thrillingly, straight up they climbed! Swifter pulled back on the yoke and choked the throttle, flipping the winged wonder over, stalling her out. Matilda squawked, tucking in her wings. To the ground they smoothly fell, dropping like a stone! Arms out, belly up. Daringly diving, the dragon and hen both, fearlessly free-falling upside-down! "Ho ho! Ha ha ha!" Winfred held up his arms wide, and squealed with delight! "Eee, I I I, O O Eye! E, O-K! E! Eee!" Roland, just held on for dear life, apparently, quoting random letters, and simply screamed! All the way down, screaming, alphabet streaming. Although uttering only a choice few it would seem.

The Teeny Tiny Dragon, thrilled to have the wind in her face again, was absolutely having herself, an absolute blast. Confident, literally flying with pure blind faith! Monoplane Matilda handled most superbly. The ole battle-tested bird, a dream machine to fly. The aerobatic dragon, obviously, is a natural borne pilot. The up-and-coming ace, surely destined to reign the skies. She felt a rush, almost like the earth was somehow calling, as they were drawing closer.

Like an old veteran at the game, the Teeny Tiny Dragon flew her charge expertly to the target. A long flat strip of clear deer trail serendipitously opened up directly ahead. Appearing all by itself apparently. She stuck the El-Zee! Unflinchingly bringing Matilda in with her nose up, flaps down, sturdy landing gear running smooth. The pint-sized pilot, thence, solidly hit the brakes. "Bawk, Bawk, Bawk, Bawk, Bawk!" Matilda's tri-ply traction chirped loud, grabbing firm. "Ah-who-ahh!" Swifter squealed with delight! She felt her belly tingling. "Nailed it!" She squeaked! Mother Gaïa was actually moved. She simply had to help out. Moving mountains, but just a little bit.

Matilda thus slowed to a screeching stop and rested for a moment. Doing what it is that a chicken does, the hen began pecking at grass, pecking at a pebble, pecking at a grub. "Baw-bawk." It was, yummy says she. The Teeny Tiny Dragon flicked out her thin purple tongue. Swifter tasted Ancient Traveler, she tasted Eleana and Zeus in the forest. She tasted home.

Hollering out loud, Swifter clicked in her heels. "Giddy-up! We're burning daylight!" Cracking her little bullwhip tail, it went snapping. "Ta-pow!" The tiny report replied. With a firm left hand on Matilda's ruby comb, Swifter raised up her right. In it, she gripped a strong and sharp, long green pine needle. Heroically, wielding it as a rapier. Into the blazing sunrise, they strode away.

Swifter observed her vision, gradually shifting. Shifting from that featureless black, fading into, blotchy shades of grey. Always a clever girl, the Teeny Tiny Dragon paused, listening closely to the whispering woods. Now, vastly more than the usual feckless meandering stream. Chatter crackled everywhere, intoning nonverbal clues, so very clear in the telling. They were subtly saying the once babbling creek, now, was a raging river, running strong, running, dangerously deep. The treacherous obstacle, wide, unavoidable, now swollen and overflooding with momentously murky, muddy brown water. They also said the Whispering Woods were about as busy as a beehive. Come to think of it. Some of those bees were busy over at Burly's place. Oh, but let's not digress. Once again, as we were. How to get back over the river? Well, that was entirely another story. "Why did the chicken cross the creek?" Vexed and perplexed, the tiny dragon deciding how and where now becoming irrelevant. Swifter paused. Her unfinished upgrades started sending her just a hint of movement.

Multitudes of shifty silhouettes suddenly surrounded them. Hundreds of blurry, skittering shadow critter things, moved about the forest everywhere! Along with glimmers from various mobs of spirits, suggested serendipity or two of softwood dryads, and many more glimpses, showing unruly schools of sprites slinking a bit on the wild side. Plus of course, milling around, the mundane, minikin, kinfolk, everybody already knew all about.

Crawling all over the swollen banks, bounding through the briars, and running along the far ridge, throngs of pixilated chromatids came creeping in, crackling, streaming live. Swifter had difficulties deciphering the show. Near whiteout conditions, her mind stormed inside with so much practically imperceptible snow.

Rapidly mending, her frosted eyes of gold and green, did see, grim grey shadows, skulking and frolicking everywhere. Birds, bats, or unidentified flappy flittering flying anomalies, leaped through the air. Soaring in grand spirals, they chased other unknown objects, squealing and squawking. Some landed on the trees, arguing! Loudly arguing, they all were! And arguing loudly, a lot! Screeching crows joined the show. They cheered and jeered from the cheap seats, way back up in the nosebleed section. It seems the Whispering Woods really was, chock full. Of shall we say, quite the questionable visitation? The forest canopy and carpets were just buzzing with life. Literally, crawling with creeping creatures and shadow critter things, better off left unseen. Swifter was nevertheless, entirely unafraid. The Whispering Woods warned like Legion. "We, are, many!" The Teeny Tiny Dragon flicked out her slender forked tongue. She growled low. "Let's roll!" There was a new sheriff in town.

Keeping watch over them, Sol cast her warmth on the earth, her bright light, guiding their way. Kicking her shining spurs in, Swifter, and her trusty bipedal mount, boldly rode off into the sunrise. "Yee! Yee!" There was far to go. There was more to see. Swifter raised her green longsword forward, pointing the way. Taking one single step, Matilda stopped abruptly. She pecked at a big black bug. "Yum yum." She clucked. Matilda blinked her beady red eyes. With a skip, she stepped another single step forward again. "Bawk? Cluck, cluck." She was looking around all hurky-jerky. The hungry hen's head bounced all about. Her persistent pecker, perpetually pecking at potential particles of protein. "Cluck, cluck, peck. Bawk, bawk, bawk!"

How long does it take a chicken to walk a quarter mile anyway? Asking for a friend.

Could this be the end? One ought to perish the very thought. Again, we shall see. Once more, into the breech!

7. Tactical Stradgety.

Omnithopters, Engineers, and Particles of Perception.

Under the warmth of the early morning sun, Matilda bobbled and wobbled steadily on. Trotting herself, one of the most ungainly of gates that there ever was for a trotter. But the scatterbrained hen did do, the very best, that any other ordinary hen, could possibly ever hope to do. Swifter, intuitively comfortable in the saddle, was confidently heading them both for home. Her trustworthy champion, pecking at the reigns. Pecking at bugs. Pecking at grass. Pecking, pecking, pecking, every other few steps. Riding gallantly, a Teeny Tiny Dragon, hardly the size of a marble, flashed wings of gossamer, billowing unfurled in the wind. Fine as filigree, flowing fully past her back, flapping bright orange, deep reds, and a dark smokey black. Fluttering flame and flickering fire well-nigh floated high, fancifully free-falling over her teensy-weensy frame.

The young dragon's playful pageantry, unfortunately, was rather short-lived. Swifter found herself ducking reflexively, not having the use or benefit of warning, as her entire wee form in a trice, scrunched down tight. Entirely of its own accord. Abruptly squishing Swifter, without permission mind you, right flat, smooth into Matilda's back. Her wonderous magic body, involuntarily moved before she was ever aware, that he was even there. She didn't like this. Not one little bit. Swifter hissed. "Omnithopters!" She didn't like this at all. A squadron of twirling and swirling wind-tossed blades suddenly fell down upon the unsuspecting pair. Springing free from the trees, several wildly spinning, ultralight interceptors descended, spiraling down, flying in a tight tornadic formation. One challenger, poised to make his move, was coming in straight for her head. He, was directly ahead, menacingly approaching a wind-whipped blade. A Valkyrie harvester, whirling and twirling on one of the spinning seeds of a maple, was eminently headed her way. The grim reaper, smoothly banked hard, right at her twelve. Lining up head-to-head, he swooped in to attack!

Gyrating in spirals, her foe aimed his lethal scythe, slicing dangerously close at her skullcap. The rotor-winged, pint-sized, poltroonish pilot, darn near decapitating her with his blind-sided sucker punch. His surprise sortie attack came out of nowhere.

Even though Swifter was still blind, he didn't stand a chance. Not really, not even close. Not against her talents. This remarkable dragon was given unbelievable gifts! Her constitution was unlike anything the Engineer, the Craftsman, the Architect, the Gameskeeper, the Mason, the Gardener, or the Author, ever made.

They got together, and with one mind, made all things possible. And to date, Swifter was their finest. By far, the most intricate in design, the most complicated in construct, and the most cleverly conceived in creation, that was ever to be fabricated, or even thought to be, or dared be brought, into a final state of fruition. And, she had lots of metaphorical fruit, yet to pick from. Possessing a lot of options, that nothing else in our universe has. Possibly, not even occurring in any single one of them! Special, sui generis, and undeniably unique. The one and only. Unlike any other, that had come before or since. Indeed, Swifter was literally made from a different kind of stuff. Literally, originated from a different kind of place. And an extremely far, far away place, to boot. One might not actually believe, how far that really is.

Nevertheless, this baby dragon had a plethora of other gifted senses besides her eyesight to utilize. She could feel quantumized bits colliding, collapsing, creating. Divining endless vibrations, harmonics, and frequencies. Swifter's mind was engineered to receive, what would normally be, imperceptibly minuscule waves and undulations, proffering up so many uncountable possibilities of potential.

The world she couldn't currently see was like that black frothing ocean during last night's storm. Quanta, the tiniest bits, each, having different potentials, are just like rain drops of differing sizes, you see. They're constantly sending out waves of possible reception. Those waves are like ripples moving on the water, within and all throughout the water. Ever in motion, forever and always. Constantly interfering, canceling, and counteracting with one another. The perception of, has each, simultaneously collapsing into potential possibilities. The outcome, having a greater proportion of these, generally popping into existence.

Kinda like Swifter when she tunnels through the æther. Swifter was designed with the ability to choose from any potential possibility. Constantly cheating and breaking the rules, she's always playing games and taking her shortcuts. She doesn't actually move herself when teleporting, she moves the empty space between herself, and that of her destination. As everything that there is in the cosmos is directly connected, with all and everything else that there is. The seemingly insignificant tiny dragon's range was nearly limitless.

Well, that's just like our entire cosmos. The ripples of quanta are tiny to the extreme to us, as we are tiny to the extreme, to the whole of the heavens. As they say. "Just a drop of water in an endless sea." As it were. Nothing more.

The short of the matter, her recent upgrades, now give the tiny dragon pup, even greater and more amazing magical powers. Swifter's fine skills already considerably ensorced, were now expertly enhanced. That, on top of her already impressive composition of divinations, sorceries, mistrials, incantations, enchantments, and the lot. Allowing her to feel, with precision, precisely where the deadly blade was at. "Directional inclination." The dragon told Matilda. "Cluck cluck, bawk!" Returned Matilda, apparently, completely disinterested.

Swifter steeled her reserve, somehow sensing where it was in the now, and where it was going to be in the next. Her mind felt how fast it was spinning, how long it was, its mass, and its velocity. She even felt its trajectory and its axial oscillations.

The fearless little dragon, bravely hacked at the reaper with her slender, long green sword, slicing him cleanly in two! She handily finished the would-be assassin. He fell tumbling to the ground, a ruin! The entire squadron fled; cowardly tails tightly tucked between their legs. Swifter sang out in triumph! "Whee-eee! Don't fear the reaper!" The tiny dragon thrust her trusty needle rapier high overhead, proudly waving it around victoriously. "Eeee!" She squealed!

Pulling firmly back on the reigns, Swifter brought her trusted mount to a halt. "Hold up Tilly." The Teeny Tiny Dragon smiled hugely. Swifter felt a brand-new confidence. She internally could tell, exactly where Matilda was. Even where, and when, her sturdy chicken feet would touch the earth, or not. She was unafraid.

Swifter flicked her forked purple tongue out. "Let's see what was there." She said to Matilda, her mind outlining the flavors tossing in the breeze. "A Wizard, a Witch, a kitty, a dog, bunches of bugs, a butterfly, a squirrel, and a frog. Ten thousand birds, a wolf, a wolf, a wolf, a wolf, a wolf, and yet, another wolf! Why it's a whole pack of them! A Wiley Coyote as well as, many, many scary little crawling things. Lots of little kitties, a giant big spider, a soft fledgling starlet, a big, big kitty, a little brown bear, a big brown bear, a troll, and a trollette. A big burly Ogre, a college of pixies, a dryad, a quick wild hare, several schools of sprites, some porcupine, and that family of the four fine red foxes." Her purple tongue forked out again. "Ambrosia, water, raging stream insanely swollen from the storm, cliff, broken trees, broken trees, broken trees, the grandaddy of all broken trees, herds of cattle, hundreds of heifers, goblins, gobblinoids, thousands of thorns filled briars, dozens of bunnies, a murder of crows, every single pine needle in the entire forest! " She could smell, taste, hear, even feel, where they all were at. Somehow, sense where they all were, and what they were doing. Along with everything else, that dwelt, on the whole of the planet.

Her entangled set of teeny magenta fins, thence, superbly super positioning her super sensitive, dark blue earbuds. They turned the deepest colors of cobalt. Who knew colors could vibrate? Yet to her, surprisingly, as a matter of fact, they do. Unmistakably, she felt all the differing hues! She heard each sound, heard each aroma, and heard each color vibrating too! Her senses, fine-tuning every single note, crystalizingly clear. Hearing, tasting, touching. Feeling all the harmonies playing. "Can you hear what I hear? Just saying." Quanta's music redefines perfection, all being conducted with absolute precision by the Composer. The little dragon thenceforth could name every drop of water, each grain of sand, and any speck of dust, along with everything else, that dwelt, aboard our good Mother Gaïa.

See, mythical music, is mysteriously in all, of everything. It's all, in those quantum possibilities, making all the magic happen. Incredibly, everything is participative in the playing, of a perfectly performed, precision masterpiece. The amazing twin's laborious efforts, are now, coming to full capacity. She envisioned in her mind's eye, more than she ever could with her blind ones.

Awakening, her conscience was stirred, her understanding, reborn. The earth herself was actually, alive! "Hello, Sweetie." Mother Earth cooed lovingly. Swifter thus met Gaïa and she was absolutely beautiful. Her possibilities were nearly endless. "I'm so very glad you're here." Mother Earth smiled. Her equator stretched, pinching together several small island chains, just a touch closer.

Suddenly lurching forward, Matilda, and quite understandably so, was off and running at the races. The slightly distracted Teeny Tiny Dragon was caught completely unaware. Now presently, being taken for a very bumpy ride. Her strong talons, instinctually clutching firmly at the urgent hen's, serendipitously convenient in location considering the current circumstances, ruby red comb.

Just a bit earlier, one ought to be aware, Matilda had smelled something supremely yummy. She, thence was hopelessly and completely spellbound. Thoroughly enchanted under its alluring call. Thenceforth, the famished hen, thus hurried herself along, skipping on headlong and headstrong. Wobbling and bobbling away, as fast as she could, churning her way, through the heart of the whispering woods. Matilda, bobbing and flapping enthusiastically, was taking them both, in the general direction of that amazing, sweet green aroma.

Gaiia smiled again! Ocean tides rose high, spreading wide with her grin, she just couldn't help it, yet, once again. She simply loves Ambrosia. Honestly, it does smell really nice.

Teeny Tiny Dragon thought she made it up, but she was sure she heard, "Buckle up buttercup." Thereafter thrashing wildly, being tossed randomly, to and fro, the fair-weather cowgirl, still in the saddle, still good to go! Swifter was rapidly closing in on that all too elusive, eight full seconds. Still riding strong into the increasingly wild ride, the bronco-busting baby dragon held on to Matilda, as she tenaciously held on to her own, calm and cool composure. Like a Professional, Bird Riders veteran at this game, she grasped firmly on to her reigns. Swifter held them tightly in her left hand, keeping her right, whipping, snapping, reaching high over her arched back. Wings flat, silver spurs raking, golden scales blazing, her entire body aching. Randomly bashed about for exactly eight seconds on the mark, her head thence, mysteriously rang with this invisible rodeo buzzer. "TA-POW!" She cracked her tail. "Made it!" Swifter was proud. She hollered out loud!

Just past the buzzer, but distinctly buzzing, from somewhere deep within her head, there came these faint, unmistakably gleeful sounds. Gleeful sounds, emanate freely from a newly minted bright blue pair of loyal rodeo fans. Who now was wildly shouting out with their overwhelming approval! "Bully! Bully I say! Bravo! Do bring in the clowns!" Winfred exclaimed excitedly! Roland roared even more, with even greater gusto, than he ever had before. "HUZZAH!, Git, Her, Done!" Winfred stood applauding. He thought her surely, the most deserved, gold buckle-winning champ of a Teeny Tiny Dragon, that there ever was. "This is how we do it!" Still cheering, he reached over and flipped a small switch beside him. That was linked to an integrated renaissance series, of Leonardo Da Vinci valves. That was when, Swifter suddenly, simply started drooling. The Teeny Tiny Dragon drooled most uncontrollably.

Swifter inhaled deep of those sweet, yet subtly soothing sensations. "Oh my! Num, num, num. That smells, so, yum,

yum, yum!" It seems the empirical sprite had turned up her olfactory receptors, just a bit. Thus, letting their enormous palace, pleasantly fill with some amazing Ambrosia aromatherapy. "Oh wow! Oh Wow!" With sweet pure delight, Swifter squealed! "Splendiferous!" Then everything, most surprisingly displayed, was unbelievably bright in her mind. Those upgrades really kicked into high gear.

To her, everything was glittering, shimmering, sparkling! The sun, so very far overhead, now blazed a dark fiery red. It seems all of the above, was silver, blue, and gold. The color of the sky I'm told. Her rainbow? Well, it was long overdue. Swifter swung her little spiky head about, sharp teensy eyes, now, slowly scanning the surroundings. Her slender purple tongue swiftly flashed out.

Her fresh senses, registered everything about them, hundreds of glowing yellow footprints, vividly radiating clues from every single critter that had passed. She totally saw what their vibrations smelt, felt, and tasted like. Their presence, is clearly visible on the ground, in a tree, and even on the shimmering flowers. "Awesomeness!" Swifter gasped in disbelief! "No way! Beautiful flowers! And, so, so, pretty!" She thought to herself. Formerly invisible, bright, and bold blossoms now formed a waving wall woven with the most unbelievable colors. Mysteriously magical, thoroughly spectacular theater, completely, filling up the glade. Climbing, crawling, up and over, and all throughout, the haunted hills, the Whispering Woods, and everywhere thereabout. Cascading galaxies flash over the earth before her. Swirling and swaying fireballs, ballet entrancingly upon the bright sparkling blooms. Otherworldly in essence, the colors, were simply, beyond belief. "Wow!" She gasped, once again. "Lookie, looky, loverly illuminations." She never, even in her wildest dreams, could possibly imagine such beautiful things ever existed! The magnificent mountain was home to millions, upon millions, of never before seen, dark matter flowers. Mysteriously metallic petals filled every nook and cranny, all blooming in the strangest of colors she could have never even imagined! Thirty trillion new Ethereal, overlapping effervescent inputs, vibrantly lit up her screens. Swifter could now see. Boy! Could she ever! Well, sort of. At the very least, it was strikingly pretty.

A means to an end. An end to a means. Simply so much, that one dragon pup, upon one day, may truly see. See truly what's been written on the lines, and what's been written or not, in those blank spaces, as one may find themselves on occasion, stuck firmly in-between...

"Swifter honey. You have got a lot yet for you to see." Gaïa was proud. Swifter was, to all intents and purposes, darn near ready. This little dragon was quite the quick young lady. Indubitably quick, in every fashion, indeed.

8. *Nine Lives of Mog.*

Light, can't stay locked, silently in a box.

"Ok. Wait, wait, wait." Just inside Mog's hollow hovel...

"Ahh-schew, Ahh-schew, Ahh -schew!" A fierce fit of sneezing, "Ah-schew!" frightfully ensues. In her current iteration, she was infamously known as Mog. Lady gobblinoid, potion-heiress, and witch doctor extra-ordinair. Mog was currently caught up in a frightful fit of sneezes. "Ahhh-schewey! Ahhh, Ahhhhhh-schew! Ah uh, ahh-schewey!" She wiped her nose with a tissue and tossed it into the fire, to wit, she was hurriedly stoking. Which incidentally, was the direct genesis of that frightful sneezing fit. Dust and soot rose steadily in ever-lofting spirals. Incineration-induced shades popped and snapped, frantically leaping away! Just vanishing from the pit, fleeing desperately for the shadows, they hid in terror of the lights! They receded quickly as Mog added bits of wood to the fire, as the firelight really hurt their eyes. Poking prime coals into position to suit her needs, thick puffs of black smoke rolled once more into the witch's wide lumpy nostrils.

"Wait! Ah-chew! Ahhhhhh, Ah-schewey!" Mog didn't like sneezing. Sneezes were never any good she believed. She had some superstitious idea that mysterious spirits can enter the body during sneezes. And anyway, she didn't really want to talk, to them. Some visiting spirits were actually, rather dull company. Somebody very special just had to come over for a visit. "That crazy wizard can come too." Her mind, always thinking far more than her recent avatar could seem to muster. She accepted the alignments as a challenge. "Ok fine! Say hi, or something. Smiling with the satisfaction of a job well done, she dropped her poker stick on the fire. Mog believed. Mog knew the path. She thought, "Oh well. Challenge, accepted."

Her meager hovel, hidden inside a massive burned-out Myrtle tree stump, was sparsely furnished. Roughhewn branches constitute the bulk of her furniture and decor. An enormous flat-topped, roughly cut, huge granite boulder, weighing well over a thousand tons, serving as her kitchen table. How she got it in there, apparently, nobody can explain. Must have taken some kind of sorcery.

Mog rubbed her nose using the sleeve of her blouse. Much, as some fires do, the fire was popping out, the occasional red ember or two. Mog just let them die out to slowly fade away on their own. Several burnt scars littering her dirt floor, bear witness to the practice. Well, she really had other, much more pressing things to do. Mog thence proceeded to hang a heavy metal, blackened iron kettle, on a long-bent hook. The witch in the woods has some serious sorceries, freshly set to cook.

The master potioneer was mumbling to somebody. Somebody, that wasn't even there. "I know. I know. I know!" Said the witch of the whispering woods. They called her worse, but only spoken of in hushed, ignorant, and frightened tones. Mostly amongst the understandable misunderstanding children from the village. The master potion-heiress was cooking, thinking, and talking carefully. "You call, or nuthin. Wait. Wait. Liz-zard... No, wait. Wiz-zard dra-gun." She irritably yanked the cover off the already warm kettle. "What? I can't stand it! You know?" Grumbling and stirring rambunctiously, she whipped the mix with a long-handled wooden spoon. Into the cauldron, she tossed a healthy handful, of fresh, green amaranth blossoms. These tasty veggies literally grew everywhere, like weeds. Tragically overlooked by many a wayward man, starving out of sheer ignorance. Their plain green flowers and slender leaves are unmistakably identified, but unfortunately unremarkable in appearance, therefore, simply passed by. Mog turned, hollering out her door. "Brother! Ran-Dhall, come here please." She asked, swiping a sweaty black lock, of greasy matted hair, over her ear with the spoon's long wooden handle. "Want some?" She said, holding out the spoon. A big glistening glob, of effervescent green goo on the end, preparing to drip to the ground, any second.

"Not really." Ducking in her door, Rhan-Dhall threw up his hands in protest." Oh no! Not again!" He was acting like a big sissy. Off, the fat drop fell, kissing the dirt with a hiss! "Come on. You know. Please. Please. Ok? Ok! Try It. Good, good, good. You like. Come here, now you try it." Pleading, Mog handed Ran-Dhall her spoon. "No, I'm good sissy. Naw, nuten, nuten naw.! Nope, Nope, Nope." Rhan-Dhall protested again. The big sissy, hairy, half-brother, was exceptionally large, even for a gobblinoid. And, gobblinoids don't really age very well. "He's been around the mountain, more than a few times" as they say in the Barrows. He honestly had nothing to lose. Judging by his scrapes and aches, he could really benefit a lot. From just a tiny taste, of the green set to brew, in the old witch's pot. Ambrosia does a body good.

Mog just shoved the spoon in his big protesting mouth. Without another obvious option, suddenly swallowing the potion, Ran-Dhall sampled the concoction. It tasted really good! "Yumm! Good as always Eirrehs." Showing her some of the old respect, calling her by her given tribal name. The very image of who Mog truly was.

She's not actually this temporary shipping box she has to endure this trip around. Her power was on the inside. Eirrehs was a creature of the light. But this earthly vessel was made of flesh and blood, achy sore, and stiff to boot. And her words were difficult, to say the least. This kind of gobblinoid does not come with proper vocalizations. Three perhaps four-word phrases at best is all any could ever do, that is until Lady Eirrehs took up residency at Mog's place. Eirrehs didn't choose Mog. Mog chose her. Mog just enjoyed the company. Eirrehs, bravely, just dealt with it. Two women, collectively commenting in one head, is bound to compound, the clearest of comprehension.

"See?... I know. Good huh? Told you." Next, she dropped slivers of sweet maple cambium, slivers of willow switches, and a bunch of fiddle head fern fronds. Stirring the viscous brew, with her wooden spoon, Mog put in a pinch of wild mint. "To please the pallet." She would say. The sorceress was brewing a potion for stamina and fortitude. "Plop! Plop!

Plop!" The surface of her sooty black cauldron was slowly simmering. Aromatic bubbles escaped, bursting with fat green splashes all over the concoction. The old crone opened a window, allowing one wisp, of a faint green vapor trail, to drift out deep into the evergreen forest. Mog was gleefully expecting company. Her anticipated company wasn't exactly expecting Mog. Those mysterious green mists did the talking, they, do the walking.

Mog had skills to pass on. But first, some sticky icky, killer green Ambrosia, freshly baked brownies, and answers. "Big? Drag-un, how big? You know? Where did she sit? No room. Drag-uns really big! I know. Aww cawap! Now what? Wait. Wait. Kit- chen table. Brother help me! " The witch insisted, as the gigantic stone slab began singing. It lifted up, levitating itself a dwarf's whisker off the floor! Thence, her living room doorway even grew wider, opening barely enough for Rhan-Dhall to shove it through. He bewailed at the task. "I can't move it, sissy. It's way too big. I ain't, ever moved, so heavy a rock." Mog laughed and just lied. "Ha ha ha! Did too! You, move it, before. You know? You know, E-Zee." Taking her word for it, even though having no recollection of the deed, he believed he had once, already moved the enormous block.

"And this is something, one has just gotta see, at least once in their life!" After one more rejuvenating taste of Ambrosia, the mighty gullible gobblinoid grunted mightily. Pushing as hard as he apparently had the last time. For Rhan-Dhall, this was easy to move. Because he believed he had already done it once before. He thought he knew, it could be done. You know? Confident pushing it around, no problem at all. Incredibly, the impossibly massive stone slowly moved. A wall of fresh earth was getting plowed away as it did so. Mog said. "Put it out." BOOM! Pile of dirt. There, that's good. No, not there, there." BOOM! Another, pile of dirt. "Put it back." BOOM! And yet another, pile by pile, of dirt. "Nope! Wait, put it here." BADDA-BING BADDA-BOOM! Therefore thrice the piles, of dirt. "Turn it." BOOM! And, a smile, of dirt. "Don't like it. What do you think? Never mind. Turn more." You guessed it, BADDA-BING BADDA-BOOM! and finally, an even bigger smile, of dirt. Mog was really pleased. "Okay thank you. See? Told you. E-Zee. Right-on, Right-on, Right-on! That's better. Right?" Rhan-Dhall felt ten feet tall, unfortunately, that was one inch shorter than he was before. Let us hope it was worth it.

Gaïa giggled. When a gobblinoid knows they can, anything is easy. But what they don't know, well, that's entirely impossible. Think about it.

The end. The end of moving any more of that massively monolithic furniture for the day. At least, for this overworked, underappreciated, entirely well-fed, somewhat dignified, kind of gobblinoid gentleman. To be continued... Or so it's been said.

9. *Ratios of Gold.*

Butterflies and Blackberries.

Eleana, Ancient Traveler, and Zeus were searching the forest around the cabin in ever-widening spirals. Spirals, exactly like those on the snail's shell, Gracie was busy swatting in the woodshed. In the process thereof, spiraling herself rather noisily around the still, cordwood unoccupied, completely empty, barren woodshed. As the search widened more and more, the trio soon were entirely headed in the wrong direction.

Last night's storm had erased, the slightest trace, of the missing pair. Even the helpful hound's keen nose, couldn't pick up the long-lost trail. Unfortunately, the sent was obviously, long since gone. Everything was washed cleanly away. It seems these particular travelers, were in for a particularly long, pivot pointing particular, peculiar kind of day. Zeus sniffed everything. Eleana worried. Traveler sweated. "Swifter!... Matilda!..." They both, called out desperately, as they both, painstakingly, rather painfully, gradually widened their ever-spiraling search. The pristine forest was wet and unpleasant. It didn't really want to be barraged through. The signs said, "You ain't supposed to be here." It seemed to intentionally put-up defenses. Masses of prickly briar patches continually blocked their path. The mean old twisted blackberries were particularly proficient at this. They grabbed and bit into the search party with nasty, wickedly sharp thorns. "Enough of this noise!" That was when the histories say, Traveler simply snapped, sharply snapping his fingers. That too is entirely another story altogether.

"Click-clank!" The agile old archmage carefully caught a pair of falling machetes. Both, tumble down dangerously from the clear blue sky. They were quickly dropped off by Norm, the cordial postman butterfly. Who in turn, straight up, smooth shot skyward! Himself, instantly soaring several meters upon releasing the tools. "Well, maybe forget something just a bit lighter the next time, my good Master Magician?" His commentary was uncharacteristically dry. Not too much of a stretch, to ponder why. In a furious flash, he feverishly flapped his fragile four, flimsy frail wings. Finally fluttering off, but barely so. Barely sucking in some of the air, don't you know? Flittering away so feebly his frustrating special delivery left him flying away, thoroughly windless.

"Here, try this. It's been enchanted so it'll cut through the forest like a hot knife through butter!" The wizard handed Eleana a machete. Eleana skeptically looked at the tool. The machete, not the wizard. Well, on second thought, one can't be too sure about that one. Anyway, it looked rather plain and unremarkable. All worn, chipped, obviously unmaintained, and totally rusted up. Kinda like, one, whose name cannot be mentioned, a certain crusty conjurer. The lady Ogre-witch, sharply swung the machete at some vines to test the rather dubious blade in question. With a hiss, a blast of sickly green vapors arose in front of her! Thick thorned vines, simply fell away! The briar patch she hacked, was cleanly sliced through! A fresh, five-foot arc, was clearly cut, easily, some three feet deep! Severed blackberry vines crumbled and sizzled. Green, airborne steam, escaped from the scene. Fleeing from the briar patch, schools of invisible phantom pixies, alongside scores of frightened forest sprites, panicked and scattered silently. Several rustling, spinning leaves, left mysteriously poignant pointers. Little leaves, simply left to lay, sweetly but discretely, pointed out the way. Such sweet secrets, each subtle little clue. Their tells, their smells, their trails, their details, they're all in the Devil, who shall have his due. Other than that, they were quite otherwise, quite undetectable. Zeus barked. The woods, as usual, barked back. Eleana laughed, incredulous. "Right on! Now we're talking!"

The dominant duo of determined trailblazers was soon making strong and steady headway. Briars crumbled to the ground. Emerald-hued steam blasted all around. The thick sizzling clouds, steadily rose up, crackling with each swing they made. Zeus then stopped moving. His black nose was twitching, sniffing at the air. His dark bushy tail was wagging wild, and his big pink tongue was hanging out, just drooling profusely. The mutt suddenly bolted away, barking. "Ambrosia!" Traveler then caught the same smell that got the dog so very worked up. The antique alchemist knew his stuff alright. That was most certainly Mog, making the lean green. Boiling a live stream concoction, long-distance connection.

Eleana started inhaling deeply. Soothing senses came flooding through her nose. "Oh wow! Something smells good! Do you smell that? Wow! I mean. Oh wow! That's really nice!" The lady Ogre-witch was firmly under its spell. Its grasp, a powerful invisible force, compelled her olfactory receptors to acquiesce. Wrought off-grid, and let loose on the wind. Ambrosia was whispering with deep wonder throughout the ether. Expertly brewed it was. Thence, the witch cast it, woven most skillfully thereunder. Subtly calling, but indubitably ringing true. Smelling sounds, those tasty, unspoken words flavored her thoughts. Ambrosia calls." Come and sup." It simply said. "Dine. Be made whole. Come, find comfort. Find needed energy." The delightful dinner truly tempted her nostrils. The powerful potion packed a punch full of promise.

Traveler then turned quick as a rabbit. Chopping at the forest with a brand-new zeal, he was moving purposefully towards that source of the altogether amazing aroma. "I know where Swifter and Matilda are gonna go! When Ambrosia calls, pretty much everything with a nose, is pretty much, gonna make a beeline for her door. Nothing they can do about it but answer, it just calls them in any way. Mog is the best master potioneer there ever was." Eleana agreed. She wiped her drooling chin and doggedly followed the wizard. Occasionally, when applicable, she widened his path with her machete.

Zeus was already halfway there. His whole body was wagging all the way. The old yellow dog zigged and zagged, eagerly bounding over and under, bushes, brambles, twigs, and snags. Quite long gone, bolting straight as an arrow shot. Determinedly running full on, intent on gobbling vast quantities of gooey green grog, and, rather obviously, bullishly headstrong. Zeus really liked mog. She had the best treats ever!

Eleana was seriously, simply, famished. And she, couldn't hardly wait. "How long is this gonna take? I'm so hungry. Can't you find a trail? Can't you go any faster? Thanks a lot, you missed a spot. How much farther? Are we getting close? I'm hungry." The wizard began daydreaming a dream to himself. "This sure is a good and sharp machete. A really useful blade. I'll bet it's got lots of other uses..." Now, another reason to hasten his travels. Gritting his teeth, he swung with a renewed purpose at the irritating pain in his neck, sticky, prickly briars. Eleana sounded, just a little, like a great big kid. "Are we there yet?" she said. He laughed, "Don't make me come back there, young lady!"

Ancient Traveler, thence spied a fat round tortoise, trudging himself along up ahead. Methodically churning his thick legs, steadily widening the gap between himself, and, his nagging competition. You know, the tortoise even won the race? Beating everyone there, by a hare. Even the wild hare, pulled up a distant second. Rather prophetic of good ole Æsop. Quite the philosopher. Seems the chap had it right, long, long ago. "Well, one could, imagine just that?"

The end. At the end of the tunnel, there's a light up ahead. Hope it's not what one usually thinks when those words are said. Anyway...

10. Cause and Effect.

Then, take a left at the fork.

Techies rejoice! Behold! Setting the standard for a whole new breed. Something strange happened to Swifter the night she lost her sight. Normally, a dragon matures slowly. You see they develop their skills slowly and gradually as they mature. Swifter, on the other hand, being unexpectedly blinded severely compromised her ability to complete her mission. Her Willowisp companions, adjusting her receiving modules, exponentially enabled her potential early on.

To start with, this little dragon came from the extremely far reaches of the ethos. Just past the anomalistic fringes. Over there, normal dragon egg clutches are very similar to a bunch of grapes. Usually, between three to six eggs on average, are lain in a lair, some crevasse such as a cavern, a mine, or a volcano. First to last, each getting smaller as they go. Every clutch varies. Some, with really big pups, the size of pumpkins. Others, down to an occasional two-bit runt or two.

Swifter came from a slightly larger batch, one of one hundred twenty eggs! So far, the largest clutch to date. Her big brother, Shaw-mwerta, the biggest dragon ever, was laid at a record-breaking size. First, always being the largest and slowest. The last, smallest, and swiftest. In all, respects. Keep that in mind. Shaw-mwerta started out super enormous. Say, like a Percheron. Not a Percheron foal mind you, but the full-grown Percheron power horse kind of enormous. Teeny Tiny Swifter, the last one of her siblings, had to be the runt of the litter. Thus, she was the tiniest, and the fastest, dragon ever made.

All dragons are made unique, and always for very specific reasons, never by accident or at random. This miniature dragon was made, state of the art. Mother Earth needed a loyal steward. She chose a dragon to represent her. The Cosmos wanted to help out Gaïa. The Powers that be, had Swifter custom crafted to order. She simply had to be small, hyperinflation and all, you see. Then they teleported her, egg and all, directly from the eleven-dimensional ether, straight to Gaïa.

Her tiny size unexpectedly altered her growth. And, she was already, extremely small. The only way to deliver a complete list of minimal requirements meant that she must be made as small as feasibly possible. Hence, her mountainous sibling receives the shortest end of the intellectual stick. Advantage, Swifter.

They created, in a positive stroke of pure genius, literally thinking outside the box, her mind. It, reached impossible distances, vast plains of folded hyperspace convolutions, composed of her brain's inner workings, securely held entangled elsewhere in the higher dimensions.

The baby dragon's entangled brain developed much faster than her wee little body did. Her ability, to change possible potential quantum outcomes, developed very early on. In fact, Swifter made that development possible during transit, when she was still an embryo floating in her egg.

She felt a sudden disturbance, a force. She simply thought, "I am, and I move." Her thoughts immediately superpositioned her matching entangled non-Euclidean processors. Her mind thence received an exceedingly higher intellect within a most critical stage of growth. "I am, and I know." She thought and so became she, fully self-aware, long before she hatched.

Arriving with great patience, the future gargantuan listened to Gaïa. Mother Earth sang sweetly for her wee sweet pea. The pint-sized pea in her green leather pod listened to the musical quiver from her liver. Both dragon and Gaïa, singing bide your time lullabies, waiting seven days and seven nights. Before Swifter toiled like a miner, for another twenty-four more, just to dig her way out of the complexes constituting that hypersphere hole, she was all quantum tangled up in.

Remember, mind you, she had the mind and emotions of just a little baby, with all the potential skills and abilities of a full-grown, very slow-to-mature dragon. In mere days, the powerful youngling was already right on the cusp of coming into her own.

Being too young to speak, she could grasp an early understanding of what people were saying, even though she couldn't say exactly what they were saying. So, she used that tongue-twisting textbook she chewed up, developing her little thought processes. With, a little help from Gaïa. Supposition in some synonymous meanings. Maybe murble in a couple other words she didn't quite yet understand. And, close enough. "Bippity boppity boo!" Just like that. "Badda-bing badda-boom!" Bold baby dragon speech beautifully began.

By the way. About that priceless Thesaurus? It's now tucked safely under cover, squirreled away in a secret cavern. It seems Swifter uncovered a rich seam of gold. Following the thick vein, she cleft through the cliff. Cutting herself a long winding pathway, paved in shining gold. Teeny Tiny Dragon, thoroughly digging her new crib. Now there's a proper lair, fit for a dragon, hidden deep under the heart of the mountain. Well, it was a much better lair anyway, with lots more room. Complete with four chambers and all.

Several shiny, lost and precious things, already had begun showing up from time to time. Swifter thought, they wanted to be with her other, really pretty magic friends, and they simply decided to move in. All by themselves. As far as she was aware, she had no hand in it.

Meanwhile, within the Whispering Woods, mayhem ensues. "Navigational assurances acquiesce." The tiny dragon suggested to Matilda. The hen's chicken brain thought she heard the great poultry calling. The spirit spoke with a nervous vibe. "Tilly, you should let me drive."

The end. Up ahead, the end of the road was patiently waiting, lurking ominously, just around the bend.

11. Legend of Running Hen.

Coyote likes chicken.

Collin, obviously being rather wily because he was a coyote and all, wisely thence went walking out for a little stroll. The coyote went on a walkabout. See how easy that one was? So much clearer than the first. The strapping young vagabond from across the pond was thoroughly enjoying the day. Well, at least more so than Trollette anyway.

Having caught himself a whiff of some awesome ambrosia drifting in the morning air, he decided crossing the flooded waters on his raft would be a good idea. Hurriedly, pushed the rickety stick boat, and he did. Quickly into the swollen stream, it slid. Himself bravely jumping aboard, thence found Collin paddling before, he could hope to change his ever-loving mind. What on earth was he thinking? Far from shore, the coyote wasn't even sure, if this idea had any fuel to shine. So, to speak. The stream, now a dark muddy river, still was probably much clearer, than his muddled-up mind at the time. Complete with crags snags and whirlpools.

It surely would make for an excellent shortcut. One can readily see, how that can easily go both ways.

Ambrosia called above it all. "How hard could it be?" It said to him. "In and out, quick and easy." He told himself. That's just the problem with ideas. One may never know how far they really are from either the shaky or the sound. Finding out which is flawed and which is right, mostly falls on the perfect vision of twenty-twenty hindsight.

"Home is that way." Swifter, the unique dragon pup, on the other hand, having advanced foresight, pointed straight at Sol. The sun, passing the buck, pointed her finger directly at Ancient Traveler and Eleana, who were on the other side of the river, going completely the other way. Chickens, obviously don't have much sense of direction at all, especially so, when sweet Ambrosia decides to call.

So here they were. Somehow, completely turned around, charging headlong through the heart of the Whispering Woods. A Teeny Tiny Dragon, clinging precariously to the stretched-out neck of a rambunctious running chicken! Swifter felt unjustly kidnapped by that aroma most unfair. Ambrosia continued calling to everything for at least a hundred leagues around. As it was still floating openly in the morning air. One scent that seemingly had them both bounding helplessly towards that frothing stream of despair. Not good. Not good at all!

Fearing an unavoidable splashdown in the immediate future all too quickly approaching, the tiny dragon pulled back on the stick, uncharacteristically, two clicks too late. The dragon thence quickly jerked the yoke. First, she pulled, yee, and yaw. Then pushing, gee, and haw. The otherwise occupied chicken completely ignored the insistent little dragon. Dead stick, no response. Swifter squealed in a near panic attack. "Deceleration! Nine, nine, nine! Post haste!" Out of her control, bird brain Matilda wouldn't, she simply couldn't, bring herself to stop and think about it. "I ain't got time for that!" The chicken only sped up all the more! Swifter was both surprised and impressed. Matilda flew incredibly smooth, streaking mere inches over the forest floor. Just her long clawed talons touched, hardly kissing the ground at all. Boy! Matilda's bony chicken legs could really run!

Before Swifter could deter the swept-up hen, they both raced up the solid trunk of a tall leaning elm. Her powerful haunches began catapulting the hen skyward, taking great leaps and strides, step by step. Matilda brazenly hurdled low-slung branches as she ran ever higher, ever quicker. Bounding, leapfrogging, left and right, she rapidly gained altitude.

The tree, an antique elm veteran quite at ease in the forward-leaning rest, made this much easier. His centuries-old bare arms, he bore proudly. Hands held hallelujah high, gracefully reaching for the sky. Having found his place, proud of his roots. His leaves were singing a joyous tune. "I shall not be moved. I know from where; my help does come. To the heavens above, I lift my eyes. For I, shall not be moved."

Skipping, jumping, flailing, Matilda accelerated, flapping hard. The wild hen came screeching out of the canopy, eventually peaking herself a full league above the nasty murky stream.

From behind Swifter's eyes... "Holy Swift!" Roland exclaimed at full volume! Swifter, Roland, Winfred, and a pair of azure blue Genies experienced zero G for the entire duration of free fall. "Wee! Kowabunga!" Winfred just couldn't help himself. This was so much fun for him. Not so much for his twin though. "Best vacation ever bro!" Roland replied, terrified! He really did not care for carnival rides. He certainly didn't care for this. Not even one single bit.

Shooting out like a cannonball shot, her momentum thenceforth leaving spinning leaves, fluttering behind, her flying behind. As it seems, lots and lots of leaves got themselves lifted up. Thusly, a trail of leaves was left lofting wide, scattering behind with the wind. "Never saw a chicken in the sky, that high." With his sharp eyes noticing the expository fowl and flora, Collin the coyote looked up a Matilda from his rickettsia raft. Way up in the sky, an airborne chicken was mysteriously streaking high. Time seemed to freeze. She was soaring way out of her league. He knew hens can't sustain flight. Not for any length of time anyway. They only fall, sometimes with style. Sometimes, not so much.

The kind coyote maneuvered his raft directly under her, in order for the chicken to easily land on the deck. Thirteen minutes later, Matilda softly touched down like a parasol on the raft. The hen had soared in spirals like buzzards do, taking her sweet precious time with it too.

Collin had made almost twenty-one meters of forward progress, and twenty-two, unfortunately, both sideways and back. He said, slightly out of breath. "Are you alright? Rest up and tell me what's going on. But now, we really must move along. Haven't you heard? Mog says to stop on by and sit a spell, there's a giant dragon supposed to show up. The entire mountain has been invited, but he can't get around like he used to. He said he just might stay at home and sit this one out. I'm headed there now. You should come with me."

"Bawk!" Matilda said thank you very much. I'd love to tag along. Nice boat. "Bawk. Bawk?" I'm a chicken. My name is Matilda. They call me Tilly. What's your name? I smelled yumm, yumms. Want some? You sound funny. You aren't from around here." Says she.

Swifter didn't talk. Quickly, the little dragon discretely vanished. She didn't teleport, she only went crystal clear, practically invisible. The little dragon stayed very quiet, very still. She wanted to know more about this giant dragon. "Impossible! It shouldn't be here. Should she be worried for her friends? Dragons eat anything they wish. Everybody knows that."

Collin heard Matilda say, "Ba-Bawk. Cluck, cluck, cluck, cackle, cackle, bawk. Bawk, bawk." That was okay with him. He liked chicken. But first, a bit of the green grog, he had a date with Mog, that lovely old crone. The hag had the best snacks around, hands down. But that too was another story.

Meanwhile, just a bit further downstream, Dhall-Tonne stood in line behind Leviathan. The tortoise, flashed past him only mere moments ago, sprinting full on the last stretch. Not bad for a bi-centurion. The ginormous turtle beat him there by a hare. Although Mr. Jack Rabbit had jumped in, and under, Leviathan, when the tortoise got himself firmly wedged in the doorway. As of present, the bulldozing turtle was trying to squeeze his fat shell through Mog's front door. Mog's house shook with his exertions. Leaves and Myrtle nuts fell. The rattle was deafeningly invasive. Absolutely bone jarring. Behind them, stretched a long line of hungry mouths to feed. Calmly, patiently, and most happily, they spread out in a golden spiral around Mog's hollow hovel. There was no need to worry. She had plenty of Ambrosia to go around. After all, a hungry dragon ought to be able to eat a lot, so she made a triple batch. Ambrosia in every bowl, every kettle, every hold, every pan, and every pot. Just in case.

A troop of rolling armadillos crashed the party. They bowled everyone over in formation. A huge shaggy beast sporting one single spiraling horn, hiding in the tree line above the palisades, just waiting, and watching. He pawed gingerly at the cliffside, sniffing the air. He could easily hear the laughter and chatter as it carried on the wind. The mythological creature, immune to Mog's master brewing, would wait around until the party was over. They really were shy and solitary creatures. So, Mog always stashes some away, just for him. He was nearly overlooked and is rarely seen. Always appearing, rather conveniently one might add, just out of sight. "Wow! That beast is one big hairy, one-horned goat. Told you so. Still, that is not, a unicorn! Just saying." Rhan-Dhall was now inside the hovel. "Mog, why?" Thought the gobblinoid.

"Don't get her wet. And don't feed her after midnight." "Now where have I heard that before?" Rhan-Dhall wondered. But, Mog just said it, so it must be true. He put the fuzzy puppet back in his cage and firmly latched the lock. Don't want another incident, that's for sure. Besides, he had to pick up Leviathan again.

The overstuffed tortoise had rolled on his back. Having eaten a bit more than enough, he got stuck, hopelessly trying to unbuckle his breeches. A trio of bunnies hopped out of the way. A Minikin's breath, from becoming crushed and stuffed themselves. One can easily see, what's not being said here. Okay fine. On with the show.

The rickety rackety raft, of sticks, poorly stacked, creaked and clicked and clacked. Its crickety, crackity stacks, creaked, cracked, and clicked some more. Those sticks so poorly stacked moaned, they groaned, threatening to tear the raft asunder. Thence, pull them all along with it, into the murky down under. Then it cracked and creaked, it clacked even more. It leaked, it creaked, it streaked, a bit too far from shore.

The Wiley Coyote simply smiled like a scoundrel without concern. "Don't worry about her. She's the fastest hunk of junk in the Palisades." Matilda agreed. Swifter, on the other hand, was not so easily impressed. "The raft was fast, but was it sound?" She had her doubts. One doubt touched her gut and said they were really picking up speed. They were about to smash on the rocks!

The chicken, full-on panicked. "Cluck the cluck, cluck!" Matilda, screeching, grabbed the dash and intuitively smashed, an imaginary brake pedal. Teeny Tiny Dragon found herself, instinctively clamping her claws down firmly. Swifter agreed, wholeheartedly. "Slow the hunk, down! Like now!" Collin calmly stirred the river bottom with a long strong pole. The well-used and apparently sound raft, smoothly swerved around the bend, taking the gentle side of the south fork. They finally slid to a halt on a sandbank. Just past the other fork, a new waterfall had cut out huge rocks. Dropping forty spans deep into the newly undercut clay cliffs. "That, was, close!" Swifter's body blushed with relief. "Whew!" Disaster, avoided!" Her magic body involuntarily turned a pale pink. A magic morning glory, thence, sprouted spontaneously. Growing right off the chicken's neck. "Well! You just don't get to see, that every day!" Remarked Collin.

Right next to the raft, lay the fallen, Grandaddy of all broken trees. For over five thousand years it had grown from the hill. At its broken base, it had a girth of over twelve meters! This was the biggest oak both Matilda and Swifter had ever seen! It must've reached two hundred meters or more in height! Hundreds of its broken branches choked out the slower side of the south fork.

Collin helped Matilda off the raft by placing her on a long limb. He hopped up beside her. His raft thence fell to pieces and drifted into the logjam, becoming locked in as well. "Hope you have insurance mate."

A smiling adorable gecko walking by encouraged the coyote. "Ah well. The Beaver can have it." Collin replied. So, he left it to Beaver, as plain as black and white. Up ahead, it was all good in the Woods. Or was it dozens dancing on Stones? Or, was it stoners dancing by the dozen? Or perhaps, a dozen donut dunkers? Still, not so clear on the nomenclature.

Anyway. On the bank, the fallen tree made for an excellent autobahn. Its long trunk ran straight at the enormous hollow Myrtle stump that was home to the Witch in the woods. There was a line of forest dwellers curving up to her pad. A myriad of invisible, desi-corporeal underlings were dancing on Mog's kitchen table. Thousands more thralls lined her halls.

It was a good thing her hovel had a permanent glammer cast over her grounds. Anyone and anything coming to visit had best behave. Peace and love filled her place till there wasn't any room for other, lesser, more base emotions. Good vibrations make good behaviors. Like good fences make good neighbors. They just wanna get along. As Mog's Ambrosia gets passed along.

Swifter smiled, and let her morning glory glow. In her bonnet, Matilda now had a pretty pink bow.

Matilda ran under anything, and anyone, in her path. The hen, launching herself over the enormous tortoise, was absolutely determined to get inside. Outside, Dhall-Tonne was being helpful. Rhan-Dhall and he was currently flipping poor old Leviathan back over. By rocking him back and forth half a dozen times, they finally got him back on his feet again.

The bunnies, Rochester, Emerson, and Monteray, had somehow escaped their hutches. They were lazily lounging against some lush long forest ferns. Their fat furry bellies, as round as Mog's heavy metal, fire-blackened kettle! Mog was holding a full bowl in hand. The name Matilda is printed on its side. Next to Mog was a twenty-five hundred liter, steaming black cauldron full to the rim with sticky green Ambrosia. The name Swifter is printed on its side. Swifter giggled. "Goody, goody, nom, nom, nums! I got this."

The end. And ending up at Mog's, ain't too bad. Nope. Ain't too bad at all. Ambrosia, it's a good thing.

12. Lost Book of Twelve Thousand Score.

Another summer of love.

Amidst a Counsel of Companions, Blank Slate was telling a jape. "Did you hear the one about, three brownies, two witches, a sorcerer, and a four-point buck?"

Inside her hovel, Mog was filling mugs, jugs, cups, and tubs, with Ambrosia as fast as she could ladle. Swifter was stuffed really full. The Teeny Tiny Dragon ate the whole thing. She even licked the sticky black cauldron clean. When finished, Swifter tried really hard, not, too, burp! She was now fat, green, bumpy, and, kind of lumpy. She had grown in girth to boot. Swollen up, to about the size of a chicken's egg. A fat, ugly, gnarled-up chicken's egg, with wings. The fattened little dragon was sitting on young master Dhall-Tonne, using his belly for a lounge. The giant Dhall-Tonne was taking a nap on the grass, his back propped against Mog's hovel, right next to the front door. Leviathan, the legendary leatherback of even now larger magnitude, somehow found a way into Mog's living room. He was seated on her crooked wooden couch. He looked like an enormously large, emerald-stitched throw pillow. Both the couch and his tight-fitting shell were creaking as he sat. The antique turtle, talking trivia to Zeus. Zeus couldn't understand even a single word of turtle, but he liked the sounds it made. Besides, the turtle's words for a good dog, sounded like, "Hey-suse-oh-my-dawg", to Zeus.

Daniel strolled through the courtyard. He was a prime four-point buck this year, and very proud of his accomplishment. He showed off his impressive fancy new antlers to everyone. He was walking with Terra, a sleek, young doe-eyed doe. She was proud of him too. The both, best friends. The dear deer were mingling words with the local Minikin family, and Briadien, a very handsome buck jackalope. Briadien, the five-point, hillbilly bunny buck, was impressed. "I knew you had what it takes!" He was saying to Daniel. A family of Martins by the creek were playing with a frisbee. That mean little freckled-faced kid, that broke a window last week, was there, doing his best, mending fences.

Ancient Traveler, Eleana, and twenty-one invisible pixie forest sprites, thence, walked up to the party. A butterfly, appearing out of nowhere, magically crashed the party!

"Norm!" Suddenly, everyone shouted his name in unison. Sometimes he wants to go, where everybody knows his name. It seems the butterfly postman had just popped in for a pint. After all, his rounds were finished for the day. All were very happy that he made it. Unfortunately, Billy, the Mountain stayed at home. His days of flagon-drinking dragons were better left off to the younger generation. Anyhow, this giant dragon he had heard so much about, never showed up. Some puny little one showed instead. It wasn't nearly as big as the rumors had it anyway. He heard a little bit about it from Trollette after she made her way there. She did tell him, about that horrible, scary spider lime thing, menacing Mog's guests. The old Troll said the witch of the woods turned it into a blue-handled lantern. "Yeah right." The mountain moaned.

Now, get ready for a spoiler alert. Here we go. Someone finally found Waldo. He was standing under a cover, in the lower left corner, by the light post, right next to Santa. If, one wanted to know. A never-prouder Chowder, the great Grue of grey, was mostly there, with his magic witch daughter, Mogdra. The powerful enchantress, an up-and-coming, whispering wood witch in her own right. Strapping young Johann, the starving artist, stopped by for a spell and some inspiration. His trusty bronco, Rusty, stood in the drive, grazing lazily on grass. Shelby the cobra, lay napping, curling out in the sun. She was stuffed so full, she looked like a long cotton mouth door sock!

Eleana gave Mog a great big hug. Mog gave Ellie, a great big mug. A big mug, with Eleana's name, etched on it as well. Eleana went over and sat on Leviathan. He was soft and comfy. Leather does hold up really well. She noisily slurped hot Ambrosia from her mug. She was absolutely famished! And, it tasted, so very good! Three Brownies sat quietly on a plate and waited. Mog handed Traveler a bowl. It too is full of the steaming green concoction.

Outside, Drooble tackled whom he thought was Gracie. Playfully, rolling her over in the grass. The fuzzy grey kitten did a buck and roll, pinning Drooble on the ground. The kitty wasn't even Gracie at all! It was Doppelganger, another kitten from the glades. But she looked just like her though. So, it was an easy mistake. Gracie was actually sleeping atop a huge pile of snoozing kittens, that was itself, over two meters in diameter and half that in height. There lay, a fuzzy little queen of the mountain. The mountain purred.

Suddenly the ground shook violently. Everyone and everything around trembled. A slumbering giant awoke and stirred. Dhall-Tonne sat up, stretched out, and slowly stood.

Swifter rolled off the giant, Dhall-Tonne's, swollen belly. The tiny dragon wasn't quite as tiny as before. Her body was all fat, and all green, and plump, very plump. She was really, pushing maximum density this time. She looked just like, a thick shining, little key west lime. Complete, with a pair of floppy green leaves.

Unceremoniously rolled in the door, the little fat bumpy lime, suddenly sprouted long black spider legs, and began scrambling noisily towards Zeus. Clickety, clacckity, her claws raked at him, click clacking, scrape scraping, six sets of wickedly sharp, long black nails on the hard dirt floor. Zeus squealed in terror. The cowardly mutt ran behind Traveler, all whimpering up, shivering uncontrollably. Himself shocked just as much, Traveler jumped back, accidentally stepping on the aforementioned, cowardly mutt. As he fell on his but, he screamed, like a little girl. That would be, both of them. They both screamed.

The mean green Dragon spider thing, in a blink, turned around! The lumpy spider thingy was looking for Eleana. Swifter thenceforth, saw Eleana turning around. Thus-forth, the Tiny, fat round limey spidey, deciding the Ogre lady witch, needs some love. The shiny spidey thing, swiftly crawled towards the lovely lady, as she turned around to see what the commotion was all about. She casually sipped from her cup of Ambrosia, curious but completely unawares.

"Ee ee! Ah Eeee!" She screamed! A giant, fat ugly green, shiny long-legged spider something, began to climb her leg, looking for love. Eleana thence, saw the giant green spider thing, thinking, poison fangs of death were actually climbing up her leg, freaking out, for real, and turned into a full-blown ninja! Fearing the worst, her legs kicked wildly and Eleana swatted like crazy at the horrible scary green spider. "High-yah! Ah-ha! Eeee! High-yah! High-yah! Ah, ah ah! Ee! Eeee-eeee!"

Swifter was a little confused, then she started calling. "My Ma, My luv Ma. Mama Ella, luv my." The green spider lime scrambled for dear life, chirped loudly, then spun wildly about. "Eeee! Eeeeee! Ah-Eee," Suddenly, feeling those teeny tiny claws all scrabbling about, right between her knees, Eleana freaked out, all the more! Thus, she panicked, running in crazy frantic circles! Spinning and waving her arms, like a spooked seagull, desperately trying to get away! The overstuffed baby dragon, just too fat to hold on, centrifugal force, shoots her smooth out! The spinning emerald UFO flat smacks Matilda, right in the back of her innocent, bobbing feathered head! A dizzy little dragon dropped to the ground with a dense squish. "Splop, splop!" She bounced, two, times!

Swifter, belly up and groaning, too full to even change color, just rolled over on the dirt floor like a wobbling wounded warrior. No, more like a wobbling billiard ball, made of jiggling green Jell-O.

That, was when Matilda, felt the love from above. "Bawk!" She ran over and hurriedly sat on Swifter, the hen, viciously protecting her overstuffed little chick, from the crazy ninja Oger witch. "Peck peck peck!" Mog jumping in was nearly panicked. She urgently waved her hands and said. "Dra-Gun Dra-Gun Dra-Gun! Wait, better Dra-Gun. Green Dra-Gun, no bug. Wait. Wait. Wait. Swif-ter Okay?" Ancient Traveler laughed and snorted. "That scared you, pretty good!" Zeus sniffed Matilda. Swifter poked her fat face out, her blinking sad eyes saying, "Are you okay? It's me! See! My love my Mama. This much!" The precious rolly poley dragon in jade attire, spread her wings as wide as she could. Then, she spread them even wider! Her eyes of frosted wizard grey, pleading with the lady, "Please love me. Gimme a hug. Let's be friends."

Eleana simply bawled like a big baby. "Swifter honey!" With boogers of love sloshing down from her cherubic nostrils, she swept up the little fat winged lime spidey thing and held Swifter close to her rosy cheek. The uncontrollable waterworks welling out thus began. She cried and she cried.

Bloodshot eyes swelling tears of relief, with a will of their own. Cascading profusely, streaming crystal-clear drops, rolled down and down, and down. The happiest of streams, freely dripping off the end, of her happy little chin. Swifter squealed and licked Eleana's cheek with joy! "Ella, Ellie Ella! My mama, mama! My, love Mama Ella!" She said, for the most part. The old wizard rubbed his nose and sniffled. Traveler tried to hide it, but then he cried just a little. Mog said. "Knock it off, ya big baby! You're fine. Swif-Ter fine. Dra-Gun better now."

"Better than what Mog?" Traveler asked, confused. "What are you talking about?" A worried Eleana demanded. "Oh God! Blind, blind, blind, blind! Swif-Ter blind. Oh God!" Said Mog. She thought Swifter still couldn't see. Mog didn't know Roland and Winfred had changed her sensory information acquisitions.

But one need not worry too much, Swifter was going to be, so much more than just alright.

But of course, Eleana cried all over again. She pulled Swifter out in front of her face, looking intensely into the Dragon's teensy eyes. They were grey, not green and gold. Eleana gasped out between her sobbing. "Oh my God! You poor little thing. Please, say you can do something Traveler."

The wizard held out his hand, letting Swifter crawl onto his scarred knuckles. He looked at the fat bumpy green dragon. He moved his hand from left to right, watching her grey eyes following his own. Swifter smiled! "She's not blind. She's different, but she can see." Traveler went over and pulled out a lemon drop from a jar sitting on Mog's counter. He tossed it at Swifter's nose, saying, "Catch!" The fat green dragon unexpectedly leaped up. She immediately bounced herself off the wall and caught the drop on the return. Carrying it in her arms like a pigskin, she flew over to Mog, landing on Mog's head.

Tossing it into her mouth with both hands, Swifter thence, crunched down on the lemon drop, turning a bright neon yellow. Now, she shone as brightly as a lightbulb. Mog's whole hovel was lit up brilliantly! Swifter's lips turned yellow and puckered up. Teeny Tiny Dragon wasn't quite so teeny anymore. But she was still tiny, and still shiny. She curled out her thin forked tongue. Her tongue tips, now whiter than the purest snow, were tightly kinking and coiling into itty-bitty springs. Her gossamer green wings turned a very bright, deep, dark, old navy blue. "Num, num, num." The baby dragon said. She waved her dual blue banners wildly about as she chewed on the sour candy. That, makes the room dance with thousands of blinding strobe lights. Brilliant crystals flashed and danced everywhere. The grey vagabond pointed, squinting, "She saw that. How else did she catch it?" Eleana stifled a sniffle. She felt better, but only a little. "What happened to her?" She quickly asked. Traveler looked worriedly at Mog. Mog said as best as she could, "Hot water. Dragon eyes hit. Fast, fast, fast! Hit hard. You know?" But Traveler and Eleana didn't know. They hadn't the slightest clue what happened to her, or what to do. "But she's gonna be okay, ain't she?" Eleana's chin involuntarily quivered up and down. She knew she was going to cry all over again. The wise old witch of the woods lovingly hugged the blubbering lady Ogre witch. Both, Gaïa and Mog together, speaking with a palpable, assuring, and healing voice said. "Dra-Gun okay. Yeah, yeah, yeah! We fix, her. Right on, right on, right on! Eirrehs, teach me. Ambrosia, fix bro-ken. Swift-ter strong. Swift-ter see, better now. Wait. Wait. Wait. Okay? Okay." The truly understanding hag, thence, called out her humongous doorway. "Brother! Come here! Help make, them, a home. Okay?" In the hovel, the hag spun therein. Mog called her brother, impatiently in again. "Hey! Brother. Brother!" She yelled out her window whilst Rhan-Dhall hurriedly came in, ducking his head as he stepped through the door. "What's up?" Says he.

Mog, all calm now, said to him. "Go get wagon. You drive home. Turtle, Leviathan. You, leave him. He stays the night. He ate, too much. Okay, him sleep." Zeus came in between them all. He pushed his nose under every hand available. He sniffed curiously at Swifter, then returned back to his conversation with the ancient tortoise. The enormous tortoise, out cold, snored like a lumbering loggerhead. Zeus wagged his tail anyway. He smiled his best. Then, Dhall-Tonne woke up. Surprised to discover, he was already standing, he darn near fell over! Catching himself instead, he stretched out then walked in with the rest, straining hard, ducking his head. "Howdy!" Says he, through his Ambrosia-tinted, green-stained teeth.

Overall, it was a grand party for one and all. One, destined for the record books! They all simply had a ball! And, wouldn't you know? In, about twenty minutes after her very first taste of Ambrosia. Swifter's eyesight? It went way better than simply returning back to normal. She, thenceforward, had the incredible ability to switch to any wavelength of a photon in existence. She could see hot and cold. She could clearly see, a single hydrogen molecule, from well over three thousand leagues. Must admit, that, is pretty darn cool! Her eyes eventually turned even brighter and clearer than they ever were before. Her golden rays and glimmering halo really came through!

Rhan-Dhall pulled the wagon around the front. It was led by Bobby, a massively mighty, magnificent Percheron! All sleek and powerfully built, his rippling coat of deep ultra-black, encasing strong sinewy muscles. His ripples of slick ebony shone flawlessly under the midday sun. Dhall-Tonne helped everybody up, then sat into the back. The wagon moaned and groaned as he settled himself in. Bobby feared the big giant, would spell the end of him. "Just a brother from another mother. Cousin, or some kind of kin." He was heard to say.

Mog waved goodbye as the group rode away. "You call, or something. Okay?" "Giddy-up Bobby. We got to make this quick." Rhan-Dhall was in a hurry. It appears he had to go help a big burly Ogre, a Troll, a blue-ribbon heifer, and a coven of cobras, round up some little lost kitties. "Now really, one must admit. This really was, getting even better! Sounds like so much fun!"

The end of the Ambrosia, the party's over. Now what to do? How about?

13. When Travelers Collide.

Wizard needs a friend.

Hello, my friend. They call me Swifter. As you can readily see, I am a dragon. Yes, here is a real dragon. Flesh and blood. I should like to share a tale with you. The take of the day when good mother Gaïa sent me his way. I was just a baby. He was the oldest creation of all the multiverse. I think perhaps all of them. The Ancient to the extreme Traveler, just sitting. Making strange magic rune scribbles. Making magic. Weaving words into a storybook that would change my life. The wizard of words was writing my story. He didn't write it for himself. He wrote it for love. I'm sharing this story with you because his love may never even know. Yet the old vagabond writes the story for them anyway. He did so, even unto his last and final day. Said the old sage on his last, knowing was it the last. Perhaps the last he might have a chance to say. "Let them remember this of me. If unconditional love was my only pay. Because of them, I was the wealthiest wizard there was made." Then we burned him on a big bonfire. Like a Viking. Everybody came to the wake. We played joyful music. We cried. We laughed and made merry. We remembered. Love flowed. It flowed like magic. Sleep thee, well fellow traveler. Sleep thee well.

14. Drooble, Prince of Nappin.

The trouble with Drooble.

So, as legend has it. It was said many years later. Much later than before, Drooble the wildcat stretched his strong lanky frame. He was tired of napping, he wanted to play. The young adult wildcat started sharpening his strong claws on the cabin wall. Soon shreds of pine lay on the hardwood. Gracie and Swifter came up behind, quietly sneaking, utterly soundless. They both, slink stealthier than a ninja's shadow. The furry grey kitten sniffed & swatted at the dark-striped stranger's long skinny tail. This frightened Drooble to no end. Shocked, the youthful kitty panic jumped smoothly sideways, right up the wall. "Mareep!" The startled trespasser, involuntarily emitted a queer squeal of surprise as he flipped out, literally.

"He, he, he!" Swifter laughed out loud. Ancient Traveler, giving up on wishing Eleana's catnapped kitties would go catch a mouse, played along and incited the trio a little bit further. "Sick him! Git 'em boy! You ain't gonna let him do that, now are you? Git 'em Drooble!"

Drooble, Gracie, and Swifter began to brawl. Playing rescue, each taking turns being the villain. The dragon was clearly overqualified. Even Drooble, Gracie's cousin, played a long distant second fiddle to the mighty magic dragon in their magic little world.

After all this time, both kitties were fully grown. The Teeny Tiny Dragon, a full three years later, on the other hand, had only just begun to grow. Still a baby, and still tiny. A magical creature of legend, and of lore, barely the size of a squirrel. She still had centuries to grow. Her extreme talents, so pronounced at such a young age, were simply beyond amazing. Her abilities were inconceivable! If she weren't such a sweetheart, Mother Earth and all her inhabitants could be, in the metaphorical, world of hurt.

Dragons actually grow up as large as mountains don't you know. Seriously, most mountains are retired dragons that are millions of years old. It's true.

Epilogue

Off to see the wizard. Just, not that one. Destiny, meet, Fate. Hope you like him.

Well, the quartet had a date. A date with Fate. The one Fate, that's known the world around, as the greatest wizard of all time! Ancient Traveler smiled at the moniker. "Greatest Wizard of all time. Balderdash! Humph!" Yes, it's true. He may be, the greatest Wizard ever born. Born, on Mother Earth that is! But nowhere near the power of an authentic O-G.

Travelers are not from our Earth. They kind of like Swifter, hale from some other sort of place. Some other sort of place, extremely, far, far away. Imagine the trillions upon trillions of galaxies that lie, between him, and his incomprehensibly distant, far away home. And, this O-G Traveler, was in fact, the very first, of any, Traveler. He, actually, discovered the Milky way. His traveling, found the much younger sorcerer, stumbling across her far-reaching horizons, over four billion years ago. But this Fate, he was only human after all. "Can't wait for you to meet him."

The eldest conjurer of all found a certain level of anonymity, most valuable. Even the greatest of all wasn't even known at all. Not to the rest of this world, or outside of his private circle of companions. Underestimation equates, to surprise, leverage, and advantage. With respect and admiration, Ancient Traveler looked at his, friendly little dragon, companion. He would never underestimate this unique traveler from another kind of world. As, she could very easily, blast him to smithereens Or simply, just send him away, without a trace! Like all those precious pretty things, that keep vanishing in the very same way, without a trace. For now, they were off to see the wizard. Traveler was in a bind, he was way behind, and he was willing to make a deal. He really needed the help of Fate this time.

The Teeny Tiny Dragon thought, "I can't wait! He, he, he! To see what Fate, has scribed himself from the sages. Find then ourselves, mayhaps, frolicking free betwixt the pages?" Even now, the ever-mindful sage, himself, pouring over the Archaic volumes. The grand ole sorcerer, pouring out his heart, pouring out his soul. Giving freely all that was so freely given. Life is a sweet precious time. Time to live. Time, to give.

Traveler, thenceforth scribbles what he believes, his mind's eye, therefore sees. With a liver that giggles, a tiny dragon that nibbles, shares her incredible journey toward destiny. Lovingly, laboriously, longingly, eagerly anticipating the first of the Ancients, recording those histories. "I can't wait in the waiting!" No telling, in the telling, what those tall tales, may yet prove themselves to be. Tucked privily away, safely under cover, already they've been written, and, strangely enough, somehow yet to be. Found in and under, in all, or in part. Buried in the open, or read aloud, out, in the yard.

Wait. Seek, and soon you shall see. The legends of a lost tome, that you were supposed to read. That's the mythical soul and heart. All a part of the art, of fairytale fables, told, about those magical days of old. One Ancient to the extreme Traveler prepares the telling pages of a nearly forgotten lore, comprising many manuals, and many volumes more. Making mayhem magically happen. Having us believe in magic, mysteriously making, and creating, the many mighty tales, of the Teeny Tiny Dragon.

"See what I mean?" Quote. "This, was, get-ting, even, better!" Unquote. More on that, later.

"Even the Gods themselves cannot help a man, should he continue to refuse the hand of opportunity." Father, Creator of all things, I truly, thank thee.

This concludes a small portion of the translated text. As the academics and research teams analyze what they have remaining, it's been said, some of this epic, apparently, continues, until...

One legend says something or other about, when no more slumbering mountains, lay remaining.

An odd preposition, with so much unfinished text, still left to lay remaining. Buried forever, under a mile of solid stone, the gold heart of Alexandria.

For now, we are at the end. Or, possibly, to be continued. In that, Fate has a big role to play. What on Earth could be locked up in that magic book of gold leaf? Inquiring minds want to know. Just for the sake of the sciences, you see?

Aloha fellow travelers. Be well. Travel well.

Printed in Great Britain
by Amazon

12058444R00097